KAROO

and other stories

FOR GAVYN FROM HIS OUPA

KAROO
and other stories

ATHOL FUGARD

davidphilip

© text Athol Fugard
© photographs Athol Fugard
© published work David Philip Publishers

Third Impression 2017
David Philip Publishers
6 Spin Street
Cape Town 8001
South Africa

First published 2005 by David Philip Publishers

ISBN: 978-0-86486-670-7

Cover and text design: Fresh Identity
Proofreader: Kathy Sutton
Typeset in 12pt (Centaur): Fresh Identity

Printed by **novus print**, a Novus Holdings company

*David Philip is committed to a sustainable future for our business,
our readers and our country.*

CONTENTS

PART I
A Karoo Directory

Buks and Joseph 3
Lukas Jantjies 9
Klonkie 35
Johnnie Goliath 40
Katie Koopman 54
Booitjie Barends 68

PART II
Fact and Fiction

Pages from a notebook 100
To whom it <u>must</u> concern 135

PART I

A KAROO DIRECTORY

By way of an author's preface, this extract from the final scene of my last play *Sorrows and Rejoicings*. Dawid is a poet, Marta the woman he loves.

DAWID [passionate and intensely alive, a sheet of paper in his hand] Listen to this!

[He plays with the names, exploring and enjoying them for their rich musicality.]

'Appolis Arries April

'Baartman Baadjies Bokbaard and Bruintjies

'Carelse

'Duimpies

'Goliath and Grootboom

'January Japhta Julies and Jantjies

'Kleinbooi

'Malgas Muggels and Meintjies

'November

'Plaatjies Persensie

'Sambok September Stuurman

'Vaaltyn Voetpad Vetbooi

'Witbooi ...'

Yes of course, names, and straight from a Karoo telephone directory. What's so wonderful about them? Come on Marta! Take a couple and roll them around in your mouth and taste them ... [He demonstrates.] ... Jantjies ... Jantjies ... Jantjies and Bruintjies ... Jantjies Bruintjies and Duimpies ... [He smacks his lips.] The taste of the Karoo ... sweet water and dry dust! Play with Arries long enough and you'll hear that little whisper of relief when a breeze stirs the leaves of the old bluegum tree at the end of a hot day. Do the same with Vaaltyn and you'll see the Karoo veld in the middle of a drought, grey and brittle. And if it's sweetness you want then play with Marta and Barends... Marta Barends! When I roll that around in my mouth I taste Karoo food, Karoo sweetness. Warm crusty brown bread just out of the oven and honey, wild aloe honey, thorn tree honey. Warm Bruin Brood en Doringboom Heuning!

Incredible isn't it ... a poem ... an almost perfect little poem, and it comes straight out of a Karoo telephone directory! One more poem for the collection! I want it to be the first one. And it comes complete with a title: 'A Karoo Directory'.

Hell Marta! This land of ours. So beautiful! But also so cruel! Sometimes I think old Eugene Marais was right in his 'Song of South Africa': She gives nothing, but demands everything. Tears, the names of the dead, the widow's lament, the pleading gestures and cries of children ... all mean nothing to her. She claims as her holy right the fruits of endless pain.

No! Don't cry. It's only a poem, Marta ... Marta Barends! ... warm brown bread and thorn tree honey ... Yes! You are all of that.

BUKS AND JOSEPH

It is winter up here now and my days usually end with a muffled-up late-night walk through the village. Lights are usually out and everyone is asleep at that hour. But not the trees, the magnificent pines and cypresses, poplars and bluegums, acacias and wild pears that line the dusty roads of the village. The sense of them alive and awake, their huge black presences magnified still further by faint starlight, is quite awesome. I have come to know and respect them individually as much as I do the people of the valley. They offer a very real companionship in that late frost-sharp hour. And they are possibly even more companionable on the warm nights of summer when the body odours of bluegum and pine, eucalyptus and resin, mingle with the lush smell of the lucerne cut that day and the scent of roses. It is during the day of course that they justify their existence because that is when they deliver something also as precious as water in the Karoo – shade!

The loss of one of these trees is felt very keenly. I've seen one or two come down from what looked like old age. And then that one dreadful storm that blasted six of them into kingdom come with lightning strikes. Worst of all was the virus that struck the cypresses about ten years back. At one stage it looked as if we were going to lose all of them, but they fought back and in the end only about ten of them succumbed.

There is of course another family of trees without which no Karoo village would be worthy of the name ... they are mostly tucked away in small orchards behind the houses ... the fruit trees – apple, plum, apricot, peach, fig and then also the quince hedges and the grape vines. In a world as harsh as the Karoo, sweetness has a very special value. The Bushmen elevated the honey bee into their pantheon of sacred animals.

I am very proud of my own orchard.

I particularly relish the pleasure of standing in the shade of my very own fig tree on a hot summer's day and looking for a ripe fig that the muisvoëls have overlooked and then eating it in the correct Laurentian fashion. And what about the children of the village? What would life be like for them without those nighttime escapades into these orchards? Was any fruit ever sweeter than that stolen? And let us not forget the birds: the muisvoëls, Red and Pale-winged Starlings, Mourning, Laughing and Red-eyed Doves, weavers and waxbills, bulbuls and barbets. What would a summer be like without them: the mad flocks of Pied Starlings, the shafted flight of a flock of muisvoëls aimed straight at a fig tree, incessant chatter of weavers ...

Their Afrikaans names — Bonthoutkapper, Witgatspreeu, Rooioogtortelduif, Lemoenduifie — are a hymn of praise to all creation.

It was early in the summer and I had already joined the muis-voëls in making a daily round of the trees and vines to gloat over the still stone-hard young fruit and bunches of grapes slowly swelling with sweetness. The signs were good. We had got through the spring without one of those devastating late frosts that can put paid to all hopes of a fruit harvest. The danger now of course was a bad hailstorm, but so far so good.

Back in the kitchen I was brewing up the first pot of coffee for the day and sorting out the ideas I had for the play I was working on when there was a knock at the back door. If there is one moment in the day when I don't need anyone in my life it is then, when I am on the point of settling down at my table for the morning session. I am so selfish about this that sometimes I pretend not to be there and just wait quietly for whoever it is to go away. But that wouldn't work this time because I had been making too much of a clatter in the kitchen. The knock came a second time and with just the right degree of timid deference to set up in me an immediate prejudice against whoever it was. Because I knew that sound so well you see. It always ushered into my life yet another sad story ... someone looking for work or wanting to borrow twenty rand to buy food or medicine, and what always made it worse was that nine times out of ten the predicaments were genuine. But not now! I prepared myself for a brusque dismissal of whoever it was on the other side of the door, and to make this very clear I put a gruff and impatient note in my voice as I opened the door:

'Ja, wie's daar?'

'Môre Master!' ... and there, hat in hand, stood my partner on the land, my friend for life, old Buks. I've told the story of our relationship in my play *Valley Song*. But Buks wasn't alone. Behind him, but with his hat still very much on his head, stood his elder brother Joseph. At seventy-eight, Joseph Jacobs was one of the more memorable figures of the valley. He was just as grey as his younger brother – Buks was seventy-two years old – but in Joseph's case that included a magnificent full beard. If you were a stranger to our world and happened to pass him on the road into the village – he lived in the little house next to the drift – it wouldn't take you too long to remember where you had seen him before: those Sunday School pictures in your youth of Moses, just down from the mountain with the tablets in his arms. Everything about Joseph reinforced the image, the slow and dignified walk and the gaze that seemed focused permanently on things beyond the sight of ordinary men.

Buks had established for himself the right to interrupt my life at any time and about anything no matter how trivial. He didn't know he had this privilege and he certainly never abused it, which made it a little easier for me to put on an air of patience while I invited them into the kitchen and we ambled through the usual Karoo pleasantries:

Ja, we must thank the Almighty that he has given us another day on the earth ... and it looks as if it is going to be a good one and how is your rheumatism today Buks and let me give you a few more of those pilletjies which are helping me with mine and yes good morning to you Joseph and would the two of you like a cup of coffee ...

It was impossible not to make the offer with the rich, hospitable aroma of freshly brewed ground coffee in the air. So two more mugs, powdered milk and lots of sugar. I also opened a packet of rusks. After a few more exchanges about the prospects for the season and a few items of local gossip – during all of which Joseph remained silent except for an occasional nod – Buks explained why they had come. He did all the talking. His brother, staring out of the window, kept his gaze fixed on those things beyond the sight of ordinary men, which on this occasion could apparently be seen through the kitchen window.

It was the year before last Master – or was it the year before that? – no, it was definitely the year before last because there had been those heavy rains in September if the Master remembers – I was busy up there at the dammetjie leading water when I saw that one of the fallen plums under the plum tree had taken root there where it fell. Ja, sommer so right there where it fell. All by itself. Isn't the Almighty wonderful that he gives us a little fruit tree like that? And for nothing! Anyway, when I first saw it I didn't think too much about it because I mean I knew it would never get through the winter which did turn out to be a bad one – does the Master remember that one? Anyway about the little plum tree, can you believe it when spring came there it was again, and what is more it added a few inches that year. Well, when I saw it there again this spring I just knew that I had to look after it. So I started giving it its share of the water and what me and Joseph want to know now is, does the Master want that little plum tree for himself or could we dig it up and plant it at his house down there by the drif?

We dipped our rusks and drank our coffee in silence for a few seconds. My two early-morning visitors realised that they had come to me with a big request because they could see from my silence that I was considering it very carefully. I was of course doing that but not in the way that they imagined. The tree was obviously going to be theirs. What I was thinking about was how to invest that moment with the dignity it deserved. Those two men, twenty years my senior, were giving me another of the profound lessons in life the village had been teaching me over the years.

There was only one thing for it: there had to be an inspection. We finished our coffee, rinsed out the mugs and left the kitchen. It was a short walk through the still dew-drenched sweet-smelling patches of lucerne growing under the fruit trees to the old plum tree at the top of the orchard and there it was as healthy a young plum tree as you were ever likely to see. After a few seconds of silent inspection, when I am sure Buks and Joseph once again imagined that I was debating parting with the tree, I looked up and spoke directly to Joseph.

'It would make me very happy Joseph if you would take this tree and plant it at your house.'

This time he spoke:

'Thank you Master.'

What I had really been thinking about during those few seconds of silence before I spoke was that that early morning encounter with the two men had come down to an exercise in arithmetic that could almost pass as a Zen Koan:

What does a small plum tree plus two old men equal? What is the common factor in fourteen inches of young life and seventy-eight years of hard living? What was it that bound the three of them together in a sacred trinity that had then spread out to include me, the orchard we were standing in and the magnificent Karoo summer's day that was unfolding all around us in bird song and ripening fruit, in the distant voices of men and women at work and children at play?

For a few extraordinary minutes it felt as if I had my fingers on the pulse of the very day itself, that I could feel the heartbeat of that powerful and mysterious force that was driving all of us, making men work, children play, birds sing and little plum trees grow.

I stayed with Buks and Joseph while they dug around the roots of the little tree, lifted it out carefully and then wrapped it up in a wet old sack. We walked together as far as the gate and there we parted, the two of them down the dusty road to Joseph's house at the far end of the village and me to my table and the new play that I had forgotten all about.

Joseph died four years later. Buks gave me the news one morning when I joined him in the akkers with a mug of coffee. I asked him about the little plum tree and why he had wanted it for his brother. He explained that when Joseph's wife Lettie had died a year earlier, Joseph had become very depressed. He had decided to ask me for the young tree because he knew that planting it would make his brother feel better.

Did it work, I asked. Oh yes, Buks said. Planting a tree did that to a man.

And the little tree?

Oh, it was growing. One day Joseph's grandchildren would eat plums from it.

Lukas Jantjies

In his seventy-fifth year, and seemingly for no reason at all, Lukas Jantjies started dreaming again. It might well be that he had been doing so all along and had just not remembered his dreams on waking, which wouldn't have been surprising given his lifelong dismissal of his dreams as totally worthless. An attitude he had adopted at the age of fourteen, when his father had been killed in a tractor accident.

Until then Lukas had been a carefree young boy playing around in the location streets and koppies like all the other klontjies his age, teasing girls and occasionally getting up to mischief that warranted a good hiding from his very strict father. As for his dreams, he and his sister enjoyed talking about them, especially at night when they lay awake in the dark in their little room, whispering away and trying to make a really good one come along that night. But with his father's death all of that changed.

Overnight Lukas became the man of the house, responsible for looking after an ailing mother and a young sister. Life suddenly became too serious for him to waste any time thinking about that strange, unreal world he and his sister had so enjoyed talking about. The years passed and he grew into a man who lived totally in the wide-awake real world, the world that he could see, and touch and hear and smell with his eyes wide open. Eventually, either from neglect or because of his indifference to them, it looked as if he had successfully rooted dreams out of his life altogether.

Now, inexplicably, in the spring of his seventy-fifth year, they had started again and, this time, there was no dismissing them.

They were so forceful that on a couple of occasions he was actually out of his bed and fumbling around in the dark for his clothes before he woke up and realised that he had been dreaming. There was an urgency to them unlike anything he had experienced before in his life. But what really made it impossible for him to ignore them was that they all took him back to the land, to the many years of his life that he had spent husbanding the earth. You would have been hard pressed to find a set of akkers in the village that he hadn't at one time or the other pushed his spade into and filled with seed. That is what he now did again in his dreams, and the urgency of it all was because the rains had come and it was time to plant. Cabbage, carrot, pumpkin, beetroot, beans and peas – all the gritty glory of their seeds was there again in his hands, lifting his heart with hope for a good harvest at the end of summer.

But when he woke up and found himself standing next to his bed in the darkened room, the emptiness of his hands made his heart as heavy as it had been light, turning all that thrilling hope into a dull ache as he crawled back into bed.

Lukas lived in an isolated little one-room cottage high up on the slopes of Van Niekerk's Kop. There was a wooden bankie outside next to his front door and, sitting there, he had a commanding view of the village down below and the valley snaking away deep into the Sneeuberg Mountains. On the day our story starts he had spent the whole afternoon sitting there, but for once he wasn't watching the life in the village below – the people like foraging ants trailing in and out of the Trading Store, the trails of dust marking entrances and exits on the three roads that connected the village to the outside world. Dark thunder clouds were building up in the sky and he was waiting for the first heavy drops to start drumming down on his corrugated iron roof. Like the winter-dry thirsty earth, he waited patiently and without complaint. And when finally it came, when the storm did break, leaving the roads in the village under three or four inches of water, he drank in the blessing as deeply as the earth itself.

That night, in the first of the dreams, he was out on the akkers with his spade planting potatoes. From then on he was kept as busy at night in his dreams as the younger men of the village were during the day with their real spades and their real seed potatoes. But they were in no sense happy dreams. In none of them did he ever experience that deep satisfaction that used to well up in him in his younger days when he was at work planting on the akkers. There was always something that went wrong and left him with a bitter, frustrated feeling when he woke up. One night it was the hole in his pocket through which all the seed he had intended planting had dribbled out on the long walk from his house to the akkers. He had to retrace his steps all the way back, with people laughing at him, scanning the ground for the tiny onion and carrot seed, bent double all the time as he tried to pick them up, until the pain in his back woke him up.

Another time he was setting up a little trellis for his beans but his hands were so stiff and arthritic he couldn't bend the little wires that were meant to tie the arched canes together. Worst of all though was the dream in which the irrigation water went mad. That one started with the windmill spinning crazily and throwing up water into the cement reservoir like never before. Lukas had opened the outlet and was leading it onto the akkers. As always it followed him like a faithful old dog as he guided it with his spade, shovelling up little walls of earth so that the water would flow to where he wanted it.

But then he realised it was all going to waste because he hadn't planted anything in those akkers. He dropped his spade and started to hurry home to fetch seeds, but when he looked back he saw that the water was still following him, all the way down Martin Street it followed him. At the church he tried to chase it back by shouting at it and throwing stones but it just kept on coming, onto the crooked little footpath that led up the hill to his cottage and then into his house and, when he lay down exhausted on his bed, it was there in the room with him, covering the floor and rising slowly ... slowly ... He woke up just in time to realise that he had started to wet his bed again.

At first he tried to dismiss his dreams as he had done in his youth and just carry on as if nothing had happened, maintaining the simple daily routine that his life had shrunk down to – a round of eating, sleeping, and in between times sitting on his wooden bankie watching the weather and seasons unfold in the valley below him. Because it wasn't as if he dreamt every night. Sometimes three or four days would pass before he found himself back on the akkers again making yet another futile attempt to plant something. He would wait apprehensively for the next one and then have to live with the frustrations of whatever had gone wrong that time. After weeks of this, of waiting apprehensively for the next dream and then living with the frustrations of whatever had gone wrong that time, the dreams began to affect his behaviour.

The first person to notice this was his widowed sister Sanna Stierman. Sanna had a house in the location and two or three times a week she would visit her brother with a little something for him to eat, usually beans and meat or mielie pap and gravy. If her ankles were too swollen for her to take on the walk to Van Niekerk's Kop, she would send the food over to him with one of the little children who were always to be found playing in the street in front of her house. Sanna had made her mother a deathbed promise that she would look after her brother. Now, after watching him carefully for some time, she finally spoke up on one of her visits.

'What is wrong Lukas? You use to live so nice and quiet up here in your little house. Now ...? I don't know what! Every day I see you drifting down to the village and wandering around like a spook looking for a house to haunt. What is wrong Boetie?'

Sanna wasn't exaggerating. Lukas Jantjies had always been known, even as a young man, as a silent loner. From the age of sixty-five, when Mrs Tilly Terblanche had paid him off as her handyman and gardener, after first helping him secure a pension, he had been almost a recluse up there on the side of Van Niekerk's Kop. Once a week he would shuffle down into the village to buy sugar, tea and bread at the Trading Store and of course at the end of every month he would be there in the pension queue at the Post Office. As far as the village's daily round of gossip and greetings was concerned, he might as well have been dead.

But that was no longer the case. Every day Lukas could now be found somewhere in the village, usually just standing and staring at a stone wall or a young man hard at work preparing an akker for planting or just sitting next to an irrigation sloot watching the running water. People began to whisper that maybe old Lukas didn't have all his little pigs in his hokkie anymore. Sanna had every reason to be concerned and to persist with her questions even though she knew there wasn't much chance of an answer from the old man sitting opposite her, spooning his mealie pap into his mouth.

'Can I go speak to the matron at the clinic for you? Maybe she's got some little pilletjies or medicine that will make you feel better. It is not right for you to be walking around so much Lukas. Heart attack if you are not careful. Ja! That is what did it to old Vossie Skaapman. What do you say Lukas? Can I go to the clinic and ask for pills?'

Lukas got up from the table with his plate in which he had left a small portion of the pap and gravy. He went outside and put it down on the ground for the old bitch to lick clean, and then settled down on the little bankie next to the front door. He noted that the two poplars in front of the Police Station were now hazy with young green growth and that all the pear trees lining the road into the village were white with blossom. It looked as if it was going to be a good season, though there was of course still the danger of a late frost. Behind him in the house Sanna went on talking at the table as if he was still sitting there with her, working her way through all the sightings of the vagrant Lukas that had been reported to her.

'And what is this now that Dorothy says she saw you the other day down on your knees drinking water from a sloot? Come now Lukas, that is mos not the right thing to do. You could go ask anybody there in the village and they would fetch you a beker of water. And what were you doing all the way down there at De Jager's lands? Booitjie Barends said he saw you there.'

Like most of the men in the village, Lukas had been a jack of all trades. In his time he had dug irrigation furrows, built stone walls, strung miles of fencing in the mountains, repaired wind-mills and turned his hand to all the odd jobbing that the life of the village needed. He had left the imprint of his handiwork everywhere and that was what he was doing now in his seemingly aimless drifting: reading the story of the life he had lived the way others could read stories from the pages of a book.

So yes, Booitjie Barends was right. He had gone all the way down to De Jager's lands and he had stood there a long time next to the charred stump of an old cypress, remembering how as a young man he had crawled into the sheep shed at the far end of the field to shelter from one of the worst hail and lightning storms the valley had ever known. Crouched in there with a flock of terrified, bleating sheep he had seen a bolt of lightning strike the massive tree and set it on fire. Then, a few seconds later, a volley of hail stones as big as walnuts had completely flattened the lucerne field. The storm lasted only a few minutes, but at the end of it every fruit tree in the valley had been stripped of its young fruit.

And yes, Dorothy was also right. There on the corner where the Police Sergeant lived, Lukas had stopped and gone down on his hands and knees to scoop up a handful of the sweet water that was flowing along the sloot and he had remembered the fourteen-year-old boy who had joined the gang of grown men digging that very sloot. That boy had worked as hard as the men. At the end of every week old Hendrik Terblanche, who was supervising the work, saw to it that there was an extra sixpence in the wages he handed over to young Lukas.

The other men knew about that extra sixpence but said nothing because like old Hendrik they knew that Lukas Jantjies was the sole support of his mother and young sister. Sitting there now on his bankie in front of his house with Sanna's voice droning on behind him, Lukas could follow with his eyes the fence that he and Willem September had strung all the way from the cemetery and up the side of the kloof. But it was the village's patchwork of fertile vegetable akkers and lucerne fields that he spent most of his time staring at. Like all true Afrikaners his great passion was the land and working it. As a Coloured man he had of course never had title to any of his own but that did not affect that passion. It was as impersonal as the land itself. He had looked after widow Theunissens's akkers, and all the others before her, as if they were his own and the akkers in turn had yielded up to him as if he was the Master. All that mattered finally in that ancient relationship between man and land was that the hands digging and planting knew what they were doing. That more than anything else was what he now ached for: one more cycle of seasons on the land. His soul needed to plant.

The old bitch, having licked the enamel plate all the way across the yard to the fence, came back and crawled between Lukas's legs into her sleeping place under the bankie. A few seconds later he felt her warm wet tongue licking his ankles. All was quiet now. Inside the house the sound of Sanna's voice had gradually dried to a dribble and then stopped all together. She was just sitting now at the table staring vacantly through the doorway, deferring for as long as she could the moment when she would have to get back onto her swollen feet and start back home.

Everything was still. For the longest time it looked as if the only thing moving was the shadow of the old pepper tree crawling slowly across the yard. The sun was still well above the koppies in the west.

———————◄○►———————

Pension day at the Post Office

Lukas takes off his hat as he steps in out of the sun to join the small queue shuffling slowly toward the counter. Young Rebeka Julies is behind it. She was born and grew up in the village and knows to greet with their names Auntie Bettie and Sister Nellie and Meneer Koopman and all the other old folk when their turn comes at the counter and to exchange a few words. And being a village girl there is no impatience in her while the now trembling and uncertain hands open ID books and hand them over. Which is as it should be because these are the hands of the mothers and fathers of village, the hands that built the village, brick upon brick, hands that baked its bread and held babies to the breast.

So it is that when Lukas stands facing her on the other side of the counter, Rebeka waits respectfully while his calloused hands carefully open the Jiffy plastic bag in which he keeps the two documents in his life: his ID book and the letter from the Department of Social Welfare saying that his application for an Old Age Pension has been granted.

As a young girl Rebeka had joined her friends in wondering about the dark, silent man who lived all alone in the little house on the side of Van Niekerk's Kop. They had learnt little more than that there had been a sad love affair that had ended with the young woman's death. Rebeka had enthralled her playmates by spinning these bare facts into romantic tales of unrequited love and abandonment. But all of that was a long time ago. There was no curiosity in her about Lukas now. The darkly handsome and silent man of her youth had aged into just another village Oupa, and the only thought in her mind as she waits patiently is that those gnarled hands look so much like the exposed roots of the old pine tree outside the Post Office.

Rebeka makes an entry in the big Pension Ledger, after which it is Lukas's turn to make his mark next to his name in that formidable looking book. That done she hands him his cheque. A polite 'Dankie Juffie' on his side and a respectful 'Okay Oupa' on hers ends the encounter. Lukas puts on his hat and leaves the Post Office.

At the Trading Store the air inside is heavy with a throat-thickening mixture of smells, among which paraffin and raw meat dominate — there is a little butcher's shop attached to the store. Bags of potatoes and onions and a few pumpkins lie around on the floor. Boetie Greyling, the owner, stands solid and square with folded arms behind a long deep counter.

There was a time when the now almost empty wooden shelves behind him sagged under the weight of the goods crowded onto them. That was when the village was still a thriving self-contained little community bustling with activity on Saturday mornings when farmers from the outlying districts came in with their wives and children to shop for supplies, collect mail, play tennis in the afternoon, gossip over a braaivleis in the evening and then sleep over for the Sunday church service. In the location life was just as full of energy and purpose. There was always work to be had for the men, either in the village or on the farms, and because of that there was always food for the wives and mothers to put on the table. And the weekly rhythm of these lives also climaxed in a Sunday service, when an unaccompanied chorus of voices rang out in praise of the Lord from the location church. If faith can be measured in decibels, the little location church was easily the equal of the other church with its organ-inflated worship.

That was all a long time ago. Ripples from the wars and depressions that changed the rest of the world forever finally reached the valley. A slow lingering malaise set in that in time drained away the life of this little community as in many other small Karoo villages. It was officially diagnosed as the Depopulation of the Platteland. In simple language that meant the village could no longer sustain the people that lived in it. One by one the sturdy, well-built houses were emptied of people and possessions, shuttered and locked up and left to their ghosts. In quite a few cases they weren't even allowed to crumble away with dignity; as people moved out, sheep and bales of lucerne moved in. And just as insidiously the shelves of the Trading Store started to empty, finally leaving only small clusters of bare essentials with a lot of space between, like a mouth full of broken and missing teeth.

That ebbing tide of life left the location stranded high and dry on the slopes of the mountain. Unlike their counterparts in the village below, the people of the location couldn't pack up and leave for the simple reason that they had nowhere to go. Their lives were as deeply rooted in the soil of the valley as the neglected vines and fruit trees behind the village's abandoned houses. And like those vines and fruit trees they too had to survive neglect. Without work there was no food to put on the table. The faith that still rang out lustily from the location church on Sundays was challenged by the hopelessness and even despair in many hearts.

In spite of the length of the counter — it is almost twice as long as the one Rebeka Julies is standing behind down the road — Boetie doesn't allow more than one person at a time to come up to it, so until he nods at you or calls your name you wait patiently against the back wall. The exception of course is if you happen to be White, in which case you go straight to the counter and are served immediately. The shelves behind the counter have a meagre stock of the packaged and canned goods that keep the location alive: pilchards in tomato sauce, apricot jam, condensed milk, the cheapest brand of instant coffee, rooibos tea, methylated spirits and candles and also a few items for medical emergencies: Grandpa Headache Powders, Vicks Vapour Rub and Borsdruppels. Apart from a couple of fly-spotted jars on the counter with stale toffees in them, there are no luxuries or temptations to indulgence on these shelves. The people who walk in here know exactly what they want. Like everything else in their lives, their shopping lists — usually only two or three items — have been reduced to essentials.

A small group has gathered in the Trading Store, waiting for the van from Graaff-Reinet with its weekly delivery of fresh bread, when Lukas walks in. There is a radio on the counter and everyone is listening to the midday news broadcast. These are the dark, troubled years of the '80s and the announcer is reporting the latest round of violent incidents in the Black townships around Johannesburg, Cape Town and Durban: police shootings with casualties, protest marches, more bannings with dire warnings from the Government that harsh measures will be taken against all agitators and troublemakers. Boetie Greyling punctuates this now daily litany of bloody unrest with cynical comments and laughter.

'That's the trouble with those Blacks up there in the north. Give them a finger and they want to take the whole land. Government is being too gentle with them. Police must now stop this rubber bullets nonsense and shoot for real.'

Boetie looks challengingly at the group on the other side of the counter. Heads nod in agreement – life would be very difficult if you landed up in Boetie's bad books. He is a man full of deep and lasting resentments, the most nourishing of which is the one he harbours against the 'brown' people whom he needs every bit as much as they need him.

The last news item is about sixteen unclaimed bodies in a police mortuary up on the Reef – men and women, victims of a recent 'Black on Black' massacre. They have still not been given their pauper's burial because the gravediggers are on strike. In the group listening to this broadcast are four men: Fiant Riet, Jannie Carelse, Riempie Jacobs and Lukas. Boetie Greyling addresses them collectively:

'There it is now my friends. Did you hear that Mr Carelse? Mr Jantjies? The answer to all your unemployment problems – kêrels! Go make yourselves into a union, do the toyi-toyi up to Brakpan, and then go dig those graves for them. They'll pay you well. Show those fools up there what a good Karoo grave looks like.'

Before Boetie can take his bit of fun any further the van from Graaff-Reinet arrives outside in a cloud of dust, and a short while later Lukas is walking home with a loaf of white bread, packet of tea, a tin of apricot jam, a tin of condensed milk and a bottle of paraffin.

For all his resentment of his dependence on the White man and his shop, Lukas had to admit that Boetie was right: the men in the location knew how to dig a grave and they had learnt how to do it the hard way. There was a layer of bedrock underlying the land on which the location cemetery stood and this had to be broken through in order to get down to the required depth of five feet, a task that could keep a team of men taking turns with the pick busy for a whole day. He was sixteen years old when Henry de Beer invited him to join the team that was going to dig a grave for his Ouma, Mrs Lettie de Beer. When his turn came to take up the pick he had confidently slung it back over his head meaning to impress the grown men standing around watching him. But when he brought it down and it struck that rock for the first time it felt as if he had fractured his spine and all the bones in his arms.

The memory of that shattering impact was still there in his body sixty years later as he sat down to rest in the shade of an old willow tree on the side of the road. There was an irrigation furrow at his feet and a strong flow of water was coursing along it down to the lucerne fields at the bottom end of the village. As so often happened when he sat watching water flowing in a sloot, Lukas's thoughts were carried away to other times, other places.

The last grave he had dug was Jannie Sambok's. It was a Saturday morning. Yes! An early Saturday morning. And autumn, still only half light when the four of them had assembled in the cemetery. That had been a hard one to dig. By the time the sun came up they were already stripped to the waist, with sweat pouring off their bodies. It took them the whole morning to get the grave ready for the burial in the afternoon and all through their digging they could hear the women wailing down at the house where Jannie was lying in his coffin on two chairs in the front room. He didn't know it at the time, but that Saturday morning was to be Lukas's last time in the cemetery for many years to come.

Sitting there in the shade of the old willow, Lukas shook his head and stood up abruptly. He picked up his little bag of groceries, stepped out into the sunlight and carried on home. For the rest of the day he kept himself busy with any little chore he could find, anything that would keep his hands and head busy. It felt as if things were being stirred up inside him up and he didn't like or trust the feeling. He sensed that it would be a mistake to sit still and start remembering again. Washing a shirt very thoroughly, he hung it up to dry on the fence; he dragged his mattress out to air and gave it a good beating with his spade; he fetched water for the house and, in the late afternoon, he gave himself a good wash. He was busy doing this when he saw Sanna labouring up the footpath with something to eat.

Like the whole valley, Sanna listened avidly to all the news broadcasts on the little radio on her kitchen table. Any newspaper that reached the village was usually days old, while television reception was impossible because of the mountains. That left the 'wireless', as old people still called it, as the only source of news about the outside world. Every lunchtime, and again in the evening, Sanna could be found at her kitchen table with a large mug of very sweet rooibos tea listening to the latest bulletin and whenever she visited her brother she served up a selection of the more interesting items together with a plate of hot food. Sanna had a suspicion that Lukas didn't always listen and in that she wasn't wrong. The stories she had carried over with her came out so garbled in her retelling that most times Lukas didn't know what they were about.

In any case, his sister's voice, droning on and on had become one of the background noises in his life that he heard from time to time but paid no real attention to, like the creaking of his roof at night when the corrugated iron sheets cooled down or a strong wind had them rattling away. His lack of interest did not stop Sanna. She needed the sound of a human voice, her own or her neighbours' or the radio announcers', the way Lukas needed the sound of his silence. On this occasion, as she ladled out baked beans on thick slices of white bread, Sanna was muddling together a story about a road accident near Uitenhage involving eleven dead sheep, drought conditions in the Eastern Cape and another riot in a Port Elizabeth township together with an item of local gossip concerning the school principal's wife — for the second Sunday in a row she had not been seen in church and everyone knew she wasn't sick. In one of the brief pauses while beans and bread went into her mouth Lukas asked his question:

'Did they say anything more about those dead ones lying up there in the Police Station?'

Accustomed as she was to his total indifference, Sanna was left speechless for a good few seconds. Lukas, meanwhile, was even more surprised than his sister. Where had the question come from? Had they been on his mind long, those eleven bodies lying in the mortuary because no one had wanted them and the gravediggers didn't want to work?

Despite Lukas's explanations it was a worried Sanna who walked back to the location a little while later. Was her brother now starting to imagine things as well? Had he got the story about the dead sheep and the township riot all mixed up? No! the time had definitely come to talk to the sister at the clinic about her brother. He needed pills or something to put a stop to all the nonsense he was getting up to lately.

———◄O►———

After Sanna left, Lukas sat on at the table brooding. His visit to the Post Office and the Trading Store had heightened the dull aching sense of uselessness he now lived with every day. There was also the story he had heard on the radio. Why did those unburied bodies keep coming back to him? He had nothing to do with those dead Black men and women. Memories of times when he had been out there on the land with his spade and a pocketful of seeds made his hands and arms twitch like the muzzle and legs of the old bitch when she chased dassies in her dreams. Eventually, he got up from the table and looked after the last few chores of the day – a drink of water for the old bitch, paraffin in his little stove so that he didn't have to fuss with anything in the morning when he woke up, and then, last of all, a counting of the money he had left to make sure he had enough to carry him through to the next pension pay-out … he didn't want to end up in debt to Boetie Greyling like most of the households in the location.

Normally this little round of housekeeping was enough to ensure a reasonable night's sleep, but when Lukas finally blew out the guttering candle stump at his bedside and lay down, he was still wide awake. The midnight hours were passed drifting between his bed – just lying there and staring into the dark – and his table where he sat and watched two little rags of moonlight move slowly across the floor. At one point he even tried sitting outside, but it was a cold night and after a few minutes he was back in his bed, trapped in the maelstrom of images that sucked him down relentlessly into his past and memories of a time he had tried so hard over the years to forget.

Lukas was twenty-three years old when he and Jannie Kleynhans had been given the job of building a fence along the north boundary of the farm Blaauwberg. Dawid Prinsloo, owner of the farm, had bought a parcel of good summer grazing up there in the mountains and was adding it to his existing farm. He had offered the job to Lukas because of his reputation as a sober and conscientious worker and left it to him to choose a partner. It wasn't a job for one man alone. The new fence would climb up high into the mountains and up there you needed a companion for more than just the labour involved.

There was a seductive danger in the loneliness of that high and empty world with its insistently whispering winds, a danger that a ruined old farmhouse bore mute testimony to. It had been built many years earlier by a young married couple who had hoped to make a life on that land. But, as the story goes, the loneliness of her life unhinged the young woman and in a fit of madness she killed her husband, stabbing him to death with a kitchen knife. Lukas and Jannie had decided to make the old farmhouse their base camp. After patching up the roof they stored their coils of wire, bags of cement, fence posts and tools in one of the crumbling rooms, and rolled out their blankets and built a small fireplace in another. It was going to be their home for a good few months. The two men worked hard because those were hard times and work was scarce. There were a lot of men with hungry families down in the valley ready to take their place if ever Prinsloo was dissatisfied with their work. So Lukas set a back-breaking pace and day by day, week by week, and, eventually, month by month, the fence, securely anchored at twenty-foot intervals and with barbed wire strands as taut as violin strings, climbed higher and deeper into the mountains.

When Prinsloo made his inspection at the end of each week there was always a grunt of approval and a parcel of freshly slaughtered mutton for the two men. But it was more than just the conscience of a good worker that kept Lukas at it with unflagging energy and had made him choose Jannie as his co-worker. Jannie had a sister – Noointjie Kleynhans – a honey-coloured beauty who everyone assumed would one day marry Lukas. She was still only a little girl when her father, old Piet Kleynhans, watching the sixteen-year-old Lukas work like a man to support his mother and sister, decided that Lukas would be the man to marry his daughter. It was in anticipation of that day that Lukas now stretched out roll after roll of fencing wire and, when the end of the month came around, asked Prinsloo to pay him his wages in a lump sum at the end of the job.

They had been up in the mountains for about four months when Prinsloo arrived unexpectedly with the news that Jannie's mother was seriously ill and wanted him at her bedside. Grateful for the good work that had been done, he suggested that Lukas might also want to go back to the village for a short break. It was a tempting invitation and Lukas wanted very much to see Noointjie, but in the end he decided to stay up in the mountains and prepare everything for Jannie's return. He was starting to get a little anxious about time. Working even harder than they had been they would still need at least another six weeks to complete the job and the nights were already getting very sharp. Once winter set in it would be impossible to go on working up there. In the end he was up there by himself in the mountains for about two weeks — Jannie's mother died a few days after his return to the village, which meant Jannie had to stay on longer to arrange her funeral.

In his boyhood, before his father's death, Lukas had been aware of strange aberrant moments in the normally sober and down to earth rhythm of his life, moments when he would drift away from reality to a place inside himself where time had a different meaning. It was more than just day dreaming. Those moments, always totally unpredictable, involved deep upwellings of a sweet sadness and a sense that if he waited long enough he would understand something very important. During those solitary two weeks in the mountains, with the sibilant insistence of the wind in his ears all the time, those moments returned and with a new and richer depth of feeling. With Jannie gone he could allow himself to sit on a sun-warmed rock and let that upwelling of emotion flood his whole being. Sitting still and watching a grass head bending in the wind, or closing his eyes and feeling that wind on his face, he could bring it on, drifting off into that place where time seemed to stop. Once, when the spell broke, he came back to himself with tears in his eyes, something that had not happened since his father's funeral when, watching his mother and sister cry, the young Lukas had fought back his own tears because he was now the man of the house and big men didn't cry. At the end of the two weeks Jannie returned with a black mourning band around the sleeve of his old jacket and the real world and real time, measured out in twenty paces between fence posts, claimed all of Lukas once again. The two men went back to work and the fence slowly but surely snaked its way ever deeper into the mountains.

From the day that Jannie returned, Lukas had a sense that something had changed between the two of them. During the day they worked together as efficiently as before, but it was at night, after they had eaten their supper and sat staring into the coals of the fire that had cooked it, that Lukas realised that Jannie was not talking to him the way he used to. This had always been a time of remembering and sharing the stories and anecdotes of their youth, taking turns to prod each other into a remembrance of times past. Lukas tried his best to get that warm camaraderie going again. With a little laugh he reminded Jannie of the time the tractor and trailer that was taking all the children to the Sunday School picnic landed up in a ditch because old Danie September who was driving it was drunk ... but all he got from Jannie was a little nod and half a smile. Lukas assumed that it was the loss of his mother that had affected Jannie and waited for him to start talking about it. But in vain. Jannie did not unburden himself.

As expected the job took another six weeks to complete. With the last anchor pole firmly planted and the last strand of wire stretched, they cleaned up the old ruin, loaded their blankets, clothes, pots and pans and tools onto the back of Prinsloo's bakkie and bounced and rattled their way down the mountain back to the village. It didn't take Lukas long to discover that it wasn't just his mother's death that had held Jannie back from the easy companionship they had enjoyed in the early months. It was Sanna who told him on his first night back home.

'Noointjie is with child Lukas. Everybody is pointing a finger at Bertus Grootboom.'

Lukas had refused to believe it, until the next day when he went around to visit Noointjie. The moment she appeared in the doorway he knew that Sanna was telling the truth. Noointjie stood there, her head lowered in shame, waiting for Lukas to say something. He didn't speak. After standing and staring at her for what seemed like an eternity to the young girl, he had turned around and walked away. Whatever he could have said to her, in judgment or forgiveness, for he himself did not know what was happening in his heart, that had been his only chance to say it. That night Noointjie went into premature labour. An ambulance had been called from Graaff-Reinet but by the time it came Noointjie had lost her child and was haemorrhaging badly. She died two days later in the hospital and was buried the following Sunday.

Lukas was not in the team that dug Noointjie's grave, nor was he in church for the service or at the graveside for the burial. From that day on the easy-going affable young man that everyone liked and had a good word for turned slowly into the withdrawn brooding Lukas Jantjies, the memory of him that would live on in the valley.

———◄○►———

It is raining heavily, a wild wind whipping stinging sheets of water across the desolate landscape. Just when it looks as if it might be letting up, another rending thunderclap overhead recharges the storm, the wind rises and the rain comes beating down with renewed fury. Lukas, drenched to the bone, stands helplessly in the middle of the graveyard, his sodden clothes flapping about him like the rags on a scarecrow. He is lost. His memory of the places where he had dug graves for his mother and Jannie Sambok and a few others bares no resemblance to the nightmarish world in which he now finds himself standing unsteadily – a miserable archipelago of grey mounds of earth in a sea of mud with home-made wooden crosses leaning drunkenly in all directions.

Eventually the storm abates somewhat and he splashes through puddles looking for his mother's grave, hoping that if he finds it he might be able to find Noointjie's, which lies near it. He has one memory to guide him. Fifty years ago, when he stood there on the side of the open grave at his mother's funeral, he had raised his eyes towards the distance in an effort to control his emotion and in those few seconds, with the church choir singing, he had noticed that the cross on top of the Mission Church lined up exactly with the beacon at the top of Van Wyk's Kop. He goes down on his hands and knees now, muttering 'Noointjie Kleynhans ... Noointjie Kleynhans ...' but none of the crosses at hand give the name back to him. Finally a huge sense of defeat overcomes him. Resisting a desire to simply sit down in the mud, he gets up and lurches to one of the scraggly pines on the side of the graveyard and leans against it for support.

Why is he here? What is he doing? He looks around. In the physical misery of that moment he has forgotten why he set out to find Noointjie's grave. Then it comes back to him: it was his dream the previous night ...

He was in a strange room and lying all around him on the floor were men and women in postures of sleep. But he wasn't fooled; he knew that they were dead. He also knew who they were: the unclaimed bodies of the Black men and women in the police mortuary somewhere up in the north. He wanted to turn away and go back to where he belonged because these Black people had nothing to do with him. But instead a terrible fascination drew him in closer. He wanted to see their faces, but their blackness was darker than the darkest night in his little room. He couldn't see anything until he came to her, Noointjie Kleynhans, the Noointjie he had tried so hard to forget for so many years, the honey-coloured skin, the sweet little mouth that even as she lay there in the pretence of deep sleep looked as if she might at any moment smile. But why was she lying there with the Black people? She was mos buried in the location cemetery. It was all wrong! She shouldn't be lying there with the Black people!

The memory of the dream engulfs him once again in a wave of despair. With one final helpless gesture Lukas leaves the thin shelter of the old pine and staggers out into the road, the wind and rain scourging him all the way home.

————◀○▶————

Sanna heard about Lukas's visit to the cemetery from Betty Malgas. Her description of him lurching from side to side like a drunken man as he staggered home through the rain — she and her children had watched him from their front room window — sent Sanna into a panic. Loading up with a pot of bean soup she hurried over to Van Niekerk's Kop as fast as her swollen ankles would carry her. She found her brother in bed, shivering and coughing under his blankets and running a temperature. Within a few minutes she had the bean soup warming up on the primus stove. It took a lot of bullying from Sanna to get the truth out of Lukas and when she finally succeeded she was dumbfounded:

'Noointjie Kleynhans's grave?'

She waited for him to say more but that was all she got. He had wanted to see Noointjie Kleynhans's grave.

'But why in heaven's name? That was mos donkey's years ago Boetie. Leave the poor girl to sleep in peace. And suppose you did find it ... what then? Did you have flowers or what? And why didn't you ask me? I would have shown you where it was. But not on a day like yesterday. Nee wragty Lukas, you were out of your mind to go there yesterday.'

It required a lot of bullying to get a few spoonfuls of bean soup and two aspirins down Lukas's throat. And while doing this, Sanna talked her way through the flood of memories that Noointjie's name had released:

'There hasn't been another one as pretty as her you know Boetie. Everybody says that Lettie Koopman is going to be Miss Beauty Queen this year but I'm telling you, if Noointjie had been alive today it would have been a different story. Haai! So young! So sad! There wasn't a dry eye next to that grave when they lowered the coffin with Noointjie and her baby inside. I hope that silly business of yours yesterday means you've finally found it in your heart to forgive her. Noointjie was a good girl Lukas. She would have made you a good wife. And when she was gone you could have had your pick of the others you know. Marie Bester! Remember her? She had eyes for you Boetie. Always asking me: "Isn't Lukas ever going to get married Sanna?" Ja! And she wasn't the only one.'

All Lukas could do was close his eyes and suffer in silence as Sanna worked her way through her memories of the young women of her youth who, according to her, had hoped to be Lukas Jantjies's wife. Out in the yard the old bitch was also listening and suffering in silence. She was waiting for the enamel plate with its little portion of something nice that she had learnt to associate with a visit from Sanna. She had to wait a long time. Sanna had a lot of memories and when she finally came out of the house and set off down the footpath it was still a while before the old bitch watching the doorway saw a trembling and blanket-draped Lukas appear with the plate.

That night his short spells of restless sleep between bouts of sweating and shivering were full of dreams about the dead. He was back on the akkers getting the ground ready for planting. Dark clouds were building up in the sky and he wanted to get the seeds into the ground before the rain came. The work was going well until he suddenly realised that they were also there, standing silently under the pear trees on the other side of the fence, watching him work ... and Noointjie was still with them. He became very angry. It wasn't right! What did she want with them? She belonged with her own people. They were Black, she was Coloured. But then, just when he had decided to go over and tell her to go back to her mother and father, the first drops of rain began to fall and he stood there not knowing what to do ... go over and talk to Noointjie or plant his seeds ... and all the time the rain was getting stronger and he was filling up with a terrible hatred of those Blacks who just carried on standing there, watching him ...

... and then he was still a young man and he was in church with his mother and sister waiting to hear Noointjie's voice ring out loud and clear above all the others when they started singing the hymns, but that never happened because there they were yet again crowding out all the familiar faces of friends and relatives ... and Noointjie was still with them ...

... and then he was back in the days when he was digging the irrigation furrows with the men with old Hendrik Terblanche standing watching them as usual and he was working as hard as hell for the sake of that extra sixpence at the end of the week until he realised that all the men down there in the ditch with him were Black ... he was working with a team of the dead ...

———————◄○►———————

Soekie Kruywagen, the Nursing Sister, accompanied Sanna on her next visit to the little house on the slopes of Van Niekerk's Kop. After taking Lukas's temperature and listening to his now racking cough Soekie had no hesitation in pronouncing him a very sick man. They got him out of bed and while Sanna sponged him down with a basin of warm water and changed his clothes, Soekie freshened his blankets and remade his bed. Then more pills and a big dose of cough mixture were got down his throat followed by a little of the fat mutton and cabbage stew Sanna had specially prepared for him. It was one of his favourite dishes. Lukas hardly registered their ministrations. When they finally left he was safely tucked in under his blankets once again. This time the old bitch out in the yard waited in vain for the enamel plate. Later than night a trail of ants led to the plate of cabbage stew on the table.

It is the late afternoon of what has been a good day in the valley, one of those gentle spring days that make it so easy to load up the heart with hope. Because of that the men had rolled up their sleeves and worked hard and happily on the akkers. In the location the air had been filled with loud laughing voices from the women gossiping and joking away at washing lines and the children playing in the streets. In other words the sort of day when people would not have looked at you askance if you had suddenly started singing while you were working. Now, in the late afternoon, as the shadows of trees start to stretch across lucerne fields and dusty roads, the men begin to put away their tools and have a last drink of water before the long walk home where the women are beginning to light fires, fill kettles and pump primus stoves in preparation for the evening meal. A serene, contented silence settles on the valley and, sitting on the bankie next to his front door, with the old bitch between his feet licking his ankles, Lukas listens to it ... in spite of his fever and bouts of delirium he has managed to wrap himself in a blanket and go outdoors. It is an eloquent silence. Listening with his heart he hears in it the story of all those days of his life when he walked home tired but fulfilled by honest labour, just as the other men are doing at that moment.

The minutes pass slowly. The silence is almost made visible when the sun finally disappears behind a koppie and the light starts to fade. It looks as if it is all over, as if the day has finally surrendered to night when suddenly, for one last lingering moment, it flares up defiantly once again, flooding the valley with a wash of soft golden light. The valley's 'golden moment' passes and night's long procession of twilight and starlight begins to make its stately entrance.

But Lukas doesn't go inside and light his lamp. He stays there on his bankie as the valley begins to fill up with darkness, watching the light of other lamps and candles starting to glow in windows in the location. He knows the scene so well. In his imagination he sits down at the table with the tired men; he sees the bright expectant eyes of the children as they watch their father and then he hears his simple words of gratitude as he says grace; he watches the mother as she cuts bread and serves food. And then finally it is his own mother standing there and it is himself and his sister sitting at the table listening to the profound piety in her voice as she thanks God for the food they are about to eat, even though there is very little on the table. But that doesn't matter because, as their mother explains, they have bread and bread is all you really need, especially if God has been so good as to also give you a little mutton dripping or apricot jam to spread on it.

'Bread is sacred children. Bread is the body of our beloved Jesus. Don't ever play with it! Don't ever waste it! Remember always that it is sacred.'

The words resonate in his head like the church bell on Sundays, echoing up and down the valley. Sacred! Yes, that is what it all is – the tired men, the patient women, the innocent children, all of them down there in the location and the food on their table even if it is only a crust of bread and a scrape of jam. The feeling inside him wells up and spills out of that little room of his imagination; his sense of the sacred floods out of him and washes over everything he can think of and see in the fading light. The whole location: the church where they worship on Sundays, the little school where the children will learn to read and write, the cemetery where his mother and Noointjie and Jannie Sambok and all the others lie and where all those now starting their evening meal will one day also lie.

And he himself. Yes, he also. And that other world down there in the valley where a few little lights show where Boetie Greyling and others like him are also breaking bread. They as well. Why had it taken him so long to see it? The completeness of it. The rightness of it. The rain falls, the men plant, the akkers yield, they eat and live and laugh and love and then finally go back into the earth. Yes! Everything was sacred. That was the understanding, the knowledge he had been so close to all his life.

And then he saw them. At first they were nothing more than shadows coming up the footpath but he knew who they were and now at last he also knew what they wanted and what he had to do and now of course Noointjie was not with them anymore. There was nothing they could say to each other because they spoke a different language, but that didn't matter because he knew at last that they were sacred and had to be buried. All was clear. All was understood. It required a huge effort to stand up and go inside and fetch his spade. He abandoned his blanket there on the bankie. The old bitch curled up in it for the rest of that night and that is where Sanna found it the next day when she felt strong enough again to visit her brother and see if he was taking the cough mixture and had stopped barking like the old dog in his yard.

They found Lukas the next day in the cemetery. The doctor said it was most probably a heart attack brought on by the digging. It was a big puzzle of course what exactly he had been doing in the cemetery. Digging his own grave? It was finally agreed that the decent thing to do was bury Lukas Jantjies in the hole he had started. A team of four young men stepped forward and finished the job and Lukas was buried there the next Sunday. It was not far from where the cross on top of the Mission Church lined up exactly with the beacon at the top of Van Wyk's Kop.

KLONKIE

It was so thin he had walked right through it before he realised it was there, hanging in the air, a trail of that sickly sweet smell that drifts away from a rotting carcass in the veld. Klonkie turned around and, sniffing like a dog, slowly walked back a few steps until he smelt it again. He knew of course what it meant. Varkie Number Two was dead. But then he had known that all along. From the moment he found the hok empty his heart had tightened and he had known what to expect. A plump little piglet running around loose in those mountains had absolutely no chance of survival. Farmers still lost sheep regularly to jackal and lynx and then there was also that pair of Black Eagles that lived at the top of Aasvoëlkrans. They wouldn't have had any problem adding a fat little varkie to their diet of dassies and haasies.

Lifting his nose slightly he waited for the vagrant breeze that was drifting around in the kloof to carry the smell of death to him once again. It was a stiflingly hot day and that little breath of air kept fainting away but eventually he had the smell again in his nose and started to follow it. It led him up the side of the kloof into an area he had never explored and, in the sand in front of a rocky overhang near the top, he found the remains of Varkie Number Two. Whatever the predator, it had made a good meal of the little pig. All that remained were a few splintered bones and what looked like a scrap of dirty rag that he recognised as a piece of the pig's skin.

Klonkie went down on his haunches, poking at the remains with a stick. He tried to imagine the little animal's last moments. If the killer had been a jackal or lynx it would have stalked the piglet; there might even have been a short chase, although the pig would not have been able to run either fast or far on the boulder-strewn slopes of the koppie. It would all have ended in a sudden pounce and the grip of sharp white teeth and claws – if it had been a lynx. The eagle on the other hand would have fallen out of the sky like a thunderbolt and locked onto the little pig's back with powerful talons. He had once seen an eagle take a dassie that way. Either way there would have been squeals. There is no way Varkie would have gone without at least a few of those silence-shredding squeals with which his kind protest the injustice of their fate. He had only to close his eyes to hear again those of Varkie Number One when his throat was cut. Ja, that was all you could do if you were a helpless little pig regardless of whether it was Klonkie's stepfather with a sharp knife at your throat or a Black Eagle on your back. There was no other way of fighting back.

Klonkie knew what he was talking about. That was the only way he would be able to deal with the beating he would get from his stepfather when he brought home the news of the pig's death. He would get that beating regardless of his innocence or whatever clever lie he could think up to defend himself. He had claimed for himself the job of looking after the pig, so if anything went wrong he was to blame. His stepfather's idea of crime and punishment was very basic, specially when it came to Klonkie. He had never overcome his resentment at having to take on the little boy in order to get the mother into his bed.

Thinking about all of this Klonkie realised that there was another possibility: that he could defer the beating by saying nothing about the pig's death and instead telling them all that Varkie Number Two was happy and getting big and fat and that he had gobbled up all the stale crusts and wilted cabbage leaves that Klonkie had brought in a plastic shopping bag. He would make wonderful gobbling noises like a hungry pig when he was telling his story and everybody would believe him. He was good at telling stories. In any case it would almost be the truth – how many times had he not stood at the side of the hok and watched both Varkie Number One and Two gobbling and grunting their way through bags of scraps. But then what? When would the truth finally come out? That was the question. Would it be better to get the hiding today, get it over and done with, or live with the prospect of it for a week or two.

With one of those leaps that his agile mind would make, the possibility of his stepfather suddenly dropping down dead presented itself. Why not indeed? That's the way Oupa Bruintjies had gone last week. It was a wonderful thought. Klonkie closed his eyes and wished for it very hard. He knew though that there was little chance of it happening. His stepfather's recurrent boast to the rest of the family when one of them was sick was that he had never once been to the clinic to see the Nursing Sister and that he had never swallowed a pill in his life. Both of these statements were untrue.

Klonkie stood up and kicked the remains of the pig into the rocks below the overhang and then looked around. Whatever animal had killed Varkie it had chosen a perfect spot to make a meal of him. The overhang went back far enough into the koppie to make a shallow cave that provided a perfect shelter for man or animal. Klonkie had no difficulty imagining himself sitting there next to a warm little fire while a mighty Karoo thunderstorm raged outside. And sleeping as well – the sand underfoot was wonderfully soft. The more Klonkie thought about it and moved around in it, the more the cave felt lived-in and comfortable. It brought back memories he had of his world when his real father had still been alive and his mother happy, memories of a safe and warm world.

He was so lost in his memories of that time he almost didn't see them – three red-ochre figures with long jointed legs and arms, elongated bodies and small heads on a rock face to one side of the cave. They were running, running so hard and fast he almost expected to see them move across the wall of the cave. Bushmen! This had been a Bushmen's cave! The tingling at the back of his neck was the same as that which he felt when he listened to a ghost story late at night, the same tingling that had run up his spine when Mr September, their school teacher, had shown them the pictures in the big book about the Bushmen. Looking at them Klonkie had, with a little shiver of apprehension and delight, seen himself, his small slit black eyes and high cheekbones, his small but lithe body, his sallow complexion. They were pictures of a reconstructed Bushman camp in a glass case in a Cape Town museum. In one face in particular – that of a young boy about his age with a bow and arrow – he saw himself more clearly than in any mirror he had looked into. The other children crowding around Mr September to see the pictures also saw it; they pointed at the museum figure and laughed and said: 'There's Klonkie!' With a pounding heart he now looked carefully around the cave for other signs of the life it had once known, but he found nothing. All that remained of that long-ago time was those three figures racing across the rock face. It was all he needed though. It was evidence that this cave had once been a home to those people. His people? Yes, his people! He had had thoughts about that when he saw the pictures in the book, but now the sense of belonging to them, of being one of them, was final.

Klonkie sat down at the opening of the cave and took out the cigarette butt and matches he had in his pocket. It was a good one, giving him six deep drags before it burnt his lips. He couldn't believe his good fortune. He could come up here and make up stories about those three running figures whenever he felt like it. He had a secret place all of his own and when he was tired of making up stories he could just sit up there at the mouth of the cave and look down at the valley. He had a splendid view of it from up there, sweeping away majestically to the south in a series of sinuous S curves, its spine the bone-dry bed of the Gatsrivier. Water didn't flow in it anymore for the irrigation dams higher up had put an end to the flash floods that used to charge down after heavy thunderstorms in the mountains.

It was Time that Klonkie felt flowing through the valley even though he couldn't have put a name to it as he sat there. The Karoo is an ancient world. Time is its real and final substance and the young boy not only felt it, he could see it as well as his eyes followed the course of the river through its snaking bends into the distance of a Karoo summer's day as hazy and uncertain as his own future. The monumental red sandstone krantzes storeyed up all along the sides of the valley heightened that sense of Time, of Time seen, because there was another pair of eyes there with Klonkie's: those of the painter of the running figures, squatting there with him in the soft sand at the mouth of the cave. He had also watched Time flow along the valley. The sense of his being there now was so strong that the young boy looked around at what he thought had been an empty cave, and smiled. It wasn't. Up here he would never be alone, he would never be lonely.

He sat on a little longer chewing a few of the wilted cabbage leaves. He emptied out the rest of the scraps on the spot where Varkie's remains had been — some animal would come along in the night and make a meal of it. By this time the shadows of the poplars down below were starting to stretch out across the lucerne field. It was time to go home. He stood up and went back for a last look at the three figures and that is when he decided that next time he came it would be with some of his stepsister's crayons so that he could add his picture of Varkie to the rock face.

It was on the broad dusty road leading to the location that he noticed that his shadow in front of him, elongated by the setting sun, looked exactly like the figures in the cave — long arms, legs and body and a small head. It made him feel very strong. He started to run. He wanted to run as fast as those three figures and he didn't care that it meant he would get the hiding from his stepfather that much sooner. He would tell the truth and live with the consequences.

JOHNNIE GOLIATH

There is hardly any trace of him left now in the village. Mention his name at one of those casual Saturday morning gatherings outside the Post Office or the Trading Store and you'd be lucky if someone remembered the little hunchback with a limp who used to make bricks in the kloof. His deformity – he was born with it – was not pronounced enough to make him truly unforgettable, like little Elsie Jacobs for example who at the age of thirty-eight was little more than waist-high. In addition, he invited no one into his life, not even on the most casual terms. His weekly visits to the village for a few groceries and a bottle of sweet wine were as brief and abrupt as he could make them. With lowered eyes, looking neither to left or right, he would wait his turn at the long wooden counter of the Sneeuberg Trading Store and, when his goods were finally stacked in front of him, put down his money – usually correct to the last cent – and leave.

The same was true of the brick works itself. The only ones, really, who knew it was up there in the kloof were the Village Management Board – who collected a monthly rental from Baasie de Beer, the owner of the enterprise – and the gang of men on the village tractor who drove past it once a week to dump rubbish in the open veld beyond. There was no other traffic. The dusty, rutted track that led to it went nowhere else. All that remains of the works now is the rusty shell of the old Pontiac that Johnnie had thought of as home for three long years.

The brickmaking itself had been a very primitive operation. At the centre of it, both literally and figuratively, stood a large forty-four-gallon oil drum. In this the raw ingredients of clay, coarse coal ash, fine charcoal and water were mixed before being shovelled into simple wooden moulds. After drying out in the sun, the raw bricks were built up around a stack of wood and then fired. The entire operation was powered by two sources of energy, Johnnie and a little donkey. Johnnie did the moulding, stacking and firing and the donkey, harnessed to one end of a long roughly-hewn bluegum pole that was connected at the other end to two wooden paddles inside the big drum, did the mixing by walking around in a circle prescribed by the length of the bluegum pole.

Around and around and around ... the paddles inside the drum, the donkey, the man. Johnnie's life was based on the pure geometry of circles and the most important, because in a sense it dictated all the others, was the donkey's orbit around the drum. He had once tried counting the number of revolutions it took the donkey to mix one load of clay. But each time, somewhere around the thirtieth revolution, he would fall into a sort of trance and wake up later to realise that time had passed and the donkey, knowing the mixture was ready, had paused in its endless journey and was waiting patiently for him to empty the drum and fill it up with another load of clay, ash, charcoal and water. A much easier bit of arithmetic was the number of drum loads it took to fill a working day. Ten. The fingers on his hands, starting with the thumb on his left hand in the early morning and ending with the pinkie on his right hand in the late afternoon. But even this bit of counting went wrong sometimes until he started using the ring from a Coca-Cola can, moving it from finger to finger as he worked through the loads of the day.

A Karoo day. Cool and sweet in that all-too-brief hour between dawn and the sun's first charge of heat and light when it rose above the koppies in the east. Then the steady and relentless build-up to the breathless heat of midday when the only sound of life in the village was an occasional call from a turtle dove in a bluegum tree. By this time about six drumloads of clay had been dealt with. Man and animal were then so exhausted that, after an hour of rest, it still took them all of the afternoon to get through the last four. The only variations in this cycle were the dusty, parching winds of spring that had every windmill in the village spinning wildly, and the stately high drama of the thunderstorms that rolled in from the west.

And then a Karoo night. Quite often the shell of the old Pontiac didn't cool off after a day of baking in the sun and when that happened Johnnie would drag his mattress out into the open and sleep under the stars. That was when he really saw them, waking up and opening his eyes in the middle of the night, shocked into immediate consciousness by the blaze of glory arching overhead. Quite often he found it impossible to go back to sleep and would just lie there on his back, wide-eyed, his mind floating away into space until the first gray light of dawn brought him back to earth. Then, as the stars faded, it was the turn of his ears: near at hand the first reluctant chirps of the mossies in the thorn tree, the last few muted hoots from an owl in the poplar grove behind the cemetery, cocks trumpeting the arrival of a new day, dogs barking in the location, an early tractor setting off for the lucerne fields and then the first human voices carrying clearly in the still air. Raising himself up on an elbow he would see the donkey waiting patiently under the thorn tree. A few minutes later his primus stove would be hissing a pot of water to the boil and a new day would be under way.

Around and around. At any point in that day he could pause and know, with reasonable certainty, that what he and the donkey were doing at that precise moment was most probably what they had been doing at the same moment the day before and would be doing at the same moment the next day and the day after that. The circle was as complete as the rut circling the drum that the donkey had tramped into the hard, sun-baked Karoo earth.

The only interruption in this cycle was of course Sunday, the Day of Rest, and then at the end of the month the arrival of Baasie de Beer in his old lorry to offload supplies for another month, load up the bricks that had been made and give Johnnie his wages – half of which he immediately handed back to Mr de Beer to give to his Ouma in the location. But these weren't really interruptions. They simply created larger circles into which all the others fitted. And so, what other men would have thought of as hell, a punishment reserved for only the most wicked of sinners, was in fact Johnnie's heaven. He had a job that paid him enough to support his Ouma back in the location, and he was left completely alone and didn't have to deal with anyone except on his Saturday morning visit to the Trading Store and Mr de Beer's visit at the end of the month. He had all the time in the world to slip into those deep reveries in which he felt so safe.

It would be wrong to think Johnnie was in any sense a slave of this little universe of interlocking orbits. From time to time strange impulses would suddenly possess him and, with a spontaneity that always set his heart racing, he would break out of the accustomed routine and do something totally unrelated to making bricks for Mr Baasie de Beer. One of the more frequent of these aberrant impulses always came in the late afternoon. No matter where they were in the actual brickmaking process, Johnnie would drop everything, unharness the donkey and climb to the top of a nearby little koppie. There he would settle down on one of the warm red sandstone boulders and wait for the women and children to return along the road down below from their daily chore of collecting firewood in the veld, the large ungainly bundles balanced delicately on their heads. It was above all the sound of their voices that he wanted to hear, their banter and laughter and, best of all, those times when one of them would be singing a song. When that happened he was filled with a feeling not unlike that induced by the bottle of sweet wine he spent his Sundays drinking.

But all of this was now going to change.

On his last visit Mr de Beer had told Johnnie that the Village Management Board had given him notice. They had decided not to renew his licence and had ordered him to shut down his brickmaking operation.

'They're jealous. That's what it is. They can't stand to see a Coloured man making a little bit of money.'

Johnnie listened in silence. He was loading the month's output of bricks onto the lorry. Normally Mr de Beer would have been there helping him, but this time he was sitting on the running board on the driver's side, fanning himself with his old hat, complaining bitterly.

'You just watch. One week after we leave one of those boere will come in here and start making bricks. And what can I do about it? Nothing. I'm mos just another old Coloured and they are White and that is the end of it. I'm telling you this country will never change. They can talk "New South Africa" as much as they like but those boere will never give us a chance.'

By the time Johnnie had finished loading the bricks Mr de Beer had still not reached the end of his complaint. After paying Johnnie and telling him to be packed up and ready to leave when he came back in a month's time, he climbed into the driver's seat, slammed the door and rattled off in a cloud of dust still cursing the boere and asking God why he let things like that happen.

Johnnie stood staring for a good few minutes at the curtain of dust left hanging in the air by Mr de Beer's departure. It took all of that time for it to settle and for Johnnie to begin to understand the significance of the news. He had evolved a simple formula for dealing with situations that challenged his understanding. He spoke to the donkey.

'Did you hear that Maatjie? The boere have told us to go. Ja. Pack up and go. One more month and then ... pack up and go. I must go back to the location, to my Ouma. Mr de Beer is going to try and sell you here in the village. Ja. It's true. End of this month it's Goodbye. Goodbye Maatjie! Goodbye Johnnie!'

And the donkey listened, standing patiently in harness with flicking tail and twitching ears while Johnnie set up the drum for another load of clay. After the last bucket of water had been poured in, the donkey, without any prompting from Johnnie, strained forward and began another endless journey around the drum.

These speeches to Maatjie that occasionally broke the deep silence of Johnnie's life went back to the one moment of crisis between the two of them. It was the day the donkey stopped working and Johnnie was to blame for it.

When he first started making bricks for Mr de Beer, Johnnie's instructions had been very specific – so much clay, so much ash, so much charcoal and so many buckets of water. As it worked out, ten drumloads of these quantities kept Johnnie and Maatjie working steadily from early morning to late afternoon. And Mr de Beer was right. It was hard work but not more than that. At the end of each month there was an impressive stack of bricks waiting for Johnnie and his boss to load onto the lorry.

The trouble started when Johnnie tried to speed up the process and finish work earlier so that he could sit up there on the koppie every afternoon and wait for the women and children to come back from the veld with their bundles of firewood. Without giving the matter much thought Johnnie increased the quantities he loaded into the drum. It was obvious that the donkey now laboured more as it walked around and around the drum, but as Johnnie saw it a donkey – it was still nameless – was just a donkey and that was the end of it. And anyway, wasn't he now also working harder? He increased the quantities still further.

The donkey survived the first week. With a lot of goading from Johnnie it got through the second. But halfway through the third it stopped, just stopped in its tracks and stood there with a drooping head, not even responding to the violent thrashing from a suddenly berserk Johnnie. In what he considered justified punishment Johnnie left it standing there in the blazing sun, without water, for the rest of the day. In the late afternoon, his rage gone and replaced by bewilderment, Johnnie unharnessed the animal and for the first time saw the red weals oozing blood where the rope halter had cut into the skin. Next morning even he winced slightly when he put the halter back on the sores. The donkey still refused to move. Another sudden rage, another thrashing, followed this time by the first flutter of panic as a whole day passed without the delivery of a single brick.

Johnnie knew he was in trouble. Instead of gaining time he was now losing it and had fallen far behind in the quota of bricks Mr de Beer would be driving out to collect in two weeks' time. He also knew that the only reason he had got the job in the first place was because Mr de Beer had fired the last man, old Gert Stierman, for always being drunk and not delivering the quota. The same fate was now approaching him.

After the last wave of panic had passed, Johnnie sat down next to the old Pontiac and stared at the drum and empty harness. He knew how to do that. If there was one thing that Johnnie could do better than most men, it was staring. A seed head of grass nodding gently in the wind, the shadow of a sandstone boulder creeping out from under it as the sun dropped in the west, clouds in the sky, the stars and moon at night ... these almost imperceptible calibrations of time were his special preoccupation. He did that now, seeing the emptiness of the harness as substantially as the donkey that had filled it. It wasn't a wasted effort. At the end of the day he knew what he had to do.

That night, when the village was asleep, he went down into one of the rich lucerne fields that surrounded the village and filled a basket with the succulent green fodder. This, and a big bucket of water, he laid out very apologetically for the donkey which had shuffled over to the thorn tree after Johnnie had unharnessed it earlier in the day and had not moved since. Johnnie's offering was not refused. But that was only half of his plan. He lay awake all night waiting for dawn and when it came he filled up the drum with just so much clay, so much ash, so much charcoal and so many buckets of water and, putting himself into the harness, he started to travel the endless circle around the drum. The donkey stood in the shade of the thorn tree munching lucerne and watching him.

Working harder than he had ever done in his life, Johnnie managed to mix, mould and lay out to dry three drumloads of clay. That night he raided the lucerne fields again. After laying out the fodder he sat down wearily under the thorn tree, his back propped up against its bole. Every muscle and joint in his body ached. He knew the donkey couldn't be put back to work so soon and the prospect of another day like the one he had just lived through filled him with despair. And for the first time in their relationship, there was the hint of another feeling. A sense of comradeship. Because he knew. Johnnie now knew what those hours in harness, under a fiery Karoo sun, were like. He fell asleep there that night, the last focus of his consciousness the comforting sound of the animal munching away.

At the end of another four days of this, watched all the time by the donkey, he had weals on his shoulders to match those that were healing slowly on the animal. The thought of yet another day defeated him. Padding up the yoke so that it was as soft and comfortable as possible, Johnnie put the donkey back into harness. It was also the first time he spoke to the animal.

'We'll take it easy today. Okay? And no more nonsense. I promise. Just so much clay, so much ash, so much charcoal and so many buckets of water ... just like Mr de Beer said.'

And then at the end of a no-nonsense day, both of them working quietly, the donkey was rewarded with a name when Johnnie unharnessed it.

'Well done Maatjie.'

Since then he had addressed the occasional monologue to the donkey and since Mr de Beer's last visit every harnessing and unharnessing of the donkey was the occasion for another speech as he tried to come to terms with the situation.

'So there it is Maatjie. The boere have told us to clear out. Pack up and go. Finish and klaar. I don't know what he's going to do

with you but it's back to the location for me, to my Ouma. Sit
there and listen to the old woman complain about this and
complain about that. Hey! Try for another job. People don't want
to give me work. I was lucky to get this one. But now ...?'

When Mr de Beer arrived to load up the last stack of bricks
and the equipment Johnny was still unaware of the thought that
had been growing in his mind. Once again Baasie, making no
attempt to help Johnnie, just sat on the running board, fanning
himself with his hat and complaining bitterly.

'And now there's also the bloody donkey. All the fuss and bother
with trying to sell it. I won't get my money back you watch. This
village is full of crooks ... the boere, our people ... all of them.
Crooks!'

The thought emerged when Johnnie told the older man that
everything was loaded up – bricks, drum, wooden moulds,
wheelbarrow and spades. As he had done on every occasion in the
past, Mr de Beer produced his old wallet and counted out
Johnnie's wages. He was about to climb back into the lorry when
Johnnie handed him back half the banknotes that had been
counted into his hand.

'For my Ouma.'

'What's this? You give it to her man. You're going back to the
location aren't you?'

Johnnie shook his head.

'I'm staying.'

'Where?'

'Here.'

'Don't be silly man. The boere have told us to clear out.'

'I'm staying.'

After a pause he held out the other half of his wages.

'And I want to buy the donkey.'

Johnnie was as amazed by his own deed and words as was Baasie
de Beer who was now beginning to wonder if something had gone
wrong with the little hunchback.

'You want to buy the donkey?'

'Yes.'

'What the hell are you going to do with a donkey?'

'I want him.'

'But for what?'

'For me.'

'Are you feeling alright Johnnie?'

Johnnie was feeling alright and he knew exactly what he was doing. Nothing Mr de Beer could say would make him withdraw the outstretched hand and banknotes. Half an hour later the old lorry ground into gear and rattled away with Baasie de Beer hunched over the steering wheel, still shaking his head in disbelief. In the rear-view mirror he caught a last fleeting glimpse of Johnnie standing quite still in the middle of that bare sunbaked patch of earth on which he and Maatjie had made bricks for two and a half years. At the last moment Baasie's conscience had made him hand back to Johnnie a twenty rand note. He made a joke of it.

'It's mos a second-hand donkey, Johnnie.'

And he had taken a message to Johnnie's Ouma: 'He says he's all right Ouma. He's doing some things there in the village. He says he will see you soon.'

After Mr de Beer's lorry had completely disappeared, Johnnie finally turned around to look at what was left of his world. He had been too busy loading up the lorry and then bargaining for Maatjie to register the finality of what had happened. He saw it now. Apart from a scattering of broken and rejected bricks, all that remained to remind him of the two and a half years that he and the donkey had laboured there was the circular rut around the spot where the drum had been. He walked over and stood in it, lowering his head and waiting for the memories. He didn't have to wait long. His body would never forget the feel of that harness chaffing up raw weals on his shoulders, his hands locked onto the bluegum pole for extra leverage and his bare feet, because that was all his lowered head could focus on, measuring out the endless journey of that circle in step after weary step. One time he had tried closing his eyes in an effort to escape the lunacy of that circle but that was just as bad because then he was travelling to ... nowhere.

He laughed.

'Never again Maatjie. It's all over. For me and for you. Ja. Finished.'

He was squatting now on the ground under the thorn tree. For the first time in his life Johnnie Goliath owned something of significance, something that other men would want and it stood there on four legs, a few feet away from him flicking away flies with its tail and twitching ears, waiting patiently for something to happen.

'I bought you Maatjie. Ja. You are mine You mos saw it all didn't you. How Johnnie paid Mr de Beer good money for you.'

And then, after a pause that stretched into the twilight:

'So now what Maatjie?'

It was a bewildering question. There were no precedents in his life to help him deal with it. The effect of ownership was a bit like that of a bottle of sweet wine, making him feel important but at the same time a little confused. What was he going to do now ... with himself and with Maatjie? He couldn't stay on in the village forever. There was no work to be found there. And Maatjie? Another long silence between the two of them stretched away to the moment when a glowing and nearly full moon floated up into the sky in the east. It had a calming effect on Johnnie. When he curled up in the Pontiac a little while later to go to sleep he knew he would find the answer to his questions.

Had anyone in the village been particularly observant that day they would have noticed a subtle change in Johnnie's demeanour when he arrived at the Trading Store. Although he still avoided all eye contact and greeted no one — after all, habits die hard — there were small hints of the self-confidence that was beginning to grow in him. He didn't, for example, hang back until everyone had been served except the children. He went straight up to the counter and waited his rightful turn. And then, in addition to the loaf of white bread and tin of pilchards, he bought a handful of toffees also. No one had ever seen him buy toffees. And at the bottle store it was the large party-size bottle of sweet wine that was wrapped up in newspaper and handed over to him.

That afternoon, he climbed to the top of his koppie and sat watching the shadows of the two thorn trees stretch slowly across the veld. And in time they appeared around a bend in the road, a ragged little army of women and children going home after another skirmish in the long battle for survival. Among them he saw the young girl with the little boy trailing behind, still too small for anything except a token bundle of kindling in his arms. How erect she was! With a pride that shamed him. How firm every step she took, turning from time to time with a word of encouragement for the little soldier struggling behind her. Johnnie took in every detail: the bare feet, the little sack of a dress exposing her honey-coloured thighs, bleached of all its colour by the sun and repeated washing, one arm swinging easily at her side, the other steadying the awkward bundle on her head.

About half way along the stretch of road that looped around the bottom of the koppie she started singing and once again the others joined in. It was a different song this time:

The stars at night
Are big and bright
Deep in the heart of Texas.

But it was her voice that he heard — loud and clear above those of the other women. They were still singing as they turned the corner and disappeared.

From the moment he heard the singing Johnnie became as still as the rock he was sitting on, hardly daring to breathe, and when they turned the corner and disappeared he closed his eyes and strained to catch the last whisper of sound as it faded away in the distance. There were pools of purple shadow now in the folds of the koppies around him. As the sun sank down to the horizon they welled up and engulfed the whole landscape. There were no clouds in the sky to dramatise the end of that day. It passed away serenely — the last flush of life in the west bleeding away into the pallor of twilight and finally the deep violet of early evening.

Johnnie opened his bottle and started to drink.

He saw the first stars arrive in the sky — the big brave bright ones first and then the little ones — and then last of all, the Queen of the Night, even more radiant than the night before. As serene as those entrances and exits in the drama of the skies, just so turbulent were the waves of thought and feeling inside Johnnie as he drank deeper and deeper into his bottle.

The girl.

Her voice.

Her pride.

Her joy.

Himself.

So what now? The decision. His pride and his gift to her.

A scramble down the mountain. Mounting Maatjie. The ride to the location. He wanted her to see him and then he would give her the donkey.

Riding up and down the roads with the little blocks of houses on each side singing 'You are my sunshine' – it was her song and when she heard it she would come out – he would come up to her and then he would give her Maatjie.

She never appeared.

Others shouted at him to shut up – one or two angry people stood in their doorways – and then the police van.

The Police Sergeant kept Johnnie locked up for forty-eight hours. It was Johnnie's first time in gaol and he was frightened. When he was finally released the Sergeant told him to get out of the village. He was a stranger – he wasn't wanted. And that was the end of it: Johnnie standing outside the Police Station blinking in the sunlight, too frightened to ask about Maatjie and what had happened to him.

It was a long walk that lay ahead of him – thirty-five miles – but of course there was always the chance of a lift.

KATIE KOOPMAN

It's a remote little village and is likely to stay that way for a long time to come, hidden away deep in the Sneeuberg Mountains. About a mile before you drive into it, the road drops suddenly into a narrow drift. This is the Gatsrivier. Every few years or so heavy thunderstorms up in the mountains will send a violent flood of water racing along its course. When that happens the village can be cut off from the outside world for days on end. Chances are, though, that the Gatsrivier will maintain its proud reputation as a Karoo river and be bone dry when you drive across it. On the other side of the drift the road climbs up again and then broadens out in a rather grand fashion with lush lucerne fields on one side and an avenue of magisterial pear and willow trees on the other. Nestling under these trees are a few scattered cottages – humble dwellings of the sort you see everywhere in the Karoo: sloping, corrugated-iron roof with a little chimney, front door with a small window on each side of it, a few chickens scratching around, a dog waiting to relieve the tedium of its existence with a bark and a good chase as you drive past and maybe a few scraps of clothing hung out to dry on a fence or a drought-stunted fruit tree. Occasionally a pot of paint has given a touch of colour to the door and window frames, but these are mostly without embellishment, as simple and unadorned as the lives of the people living behind them.

If you'd visited the village for the first time about ten years ago one house in particular would have caught your eye as your drove past, the third one on the right as you came up out of the drift. Even if you'd been in a hurry, something about it would have made you look up into your rear-view mirror for another glimpse of it through the clouds of dust billowing up behind your car. In most respects it would have appeared to be very much like all the others except for one unusual feature: the dark green shutters on all the windows. Apart from being incongruous on a labourer's cottage, they gave it that subtle air of lidded secrecy that made you want to see it again. All the other cottages had simple curtains in their windows. You wouldn't have thought twice about stopping in front of one of them, knocking on the front door and asking if you were on the right road to Boet van Heerden's farm or wherever you were headed. And someone with a face as frank and honest as that of the house itself would have tried to help you on your way.

You would have hesitated however before going up to the little house with the shutters. For some reason it did not invite a casual or unexpected knock on the front door. If you ignored this feeling and knocked, the door would have opened after a few seconds, slowly and only partly, and you would have been greeted by a little old woman – at a guess deep into her seventies – with a doek on her head, who would have told you in a soft voice that you were indeed on the right road to Baas van Heerden's farm.

'Just keep straight on Master ... the name-board is on the side of the road.'

As you drove away you might also have been struck by a certain resemblance between the lined face and lowered eyes under the doek and the shuttered secrecy of the house itself. Its owner, the person you had just spoken to, was Katie Koopman. The house was hers, as were its secrets.

Katie had been widowed for about forty years. Her husband, Jannie Koopman, had earned a living as the village handyman – if your windmill wasn't pumping up water, your roof was leaking, your fence needing mending, Jannie was the man you went looking for. He died from a heart attack when he and Katie were still quite young, leaving Katie with one child, a little girl, Marie. For as far back as the old people could remember there had always been only one child in each generation in Katie's family, and all of them girls.

They said in the location that God had given each generation just one seed to plant, but that they were special seeds because all of them grew into beautiful women.

That was certainly true of Katie as a young woman and her daughter Marie kept up the tradition. When her time came to say 'Yes', the lucky man was Apools Olifant, caretaker of the White church in the village. Among his responsibilities was one that gave him very special status in the community: he pumped the organ on Sundays so that Mrs de Bruyn could translate into solemn, dark chords the dominee's message of damnation for all unrepentant sinners. As the years passed it began to look as if Marie was going to break the family tradition by being childless, but in her forty-fourth year there it was again, a 'laat lammetjie', a late lamb. She was christened Yolanda, but 'Lammetjie' was the name her mother called from the doorway when supper was ready, and 'Lammetjie' was the name her playmates used in their games in the streets of the location.

Our story really starts all the way back in the past with Katie Koopman's mother, the beautiful Susanna Aries who was the first in that long line of one-child families. By the time she was sixteen years old she was already a striking young woman, her bright black eyes, high cheek bones and honey-coloured skin a living reminder of the people who had lived in those mountains for centuries before any others. And Sanna carried herself accordingly. It was as if she knew that hers was an ancient and indisputable claim to the land she walked on. There wasn't a young man in the location who hadn't dreamt about her proud and provocative young body. So it was no real surprise or shock to anyone when it became obvious that she was carrying a child.

Over the years there had been many love children in the location and it was quietly accepted that there would be a few more in the years to come. The location folk are realists; they know how easy it is for the hot blood to drown out the Sunday sermon. What made Susanna's story different is that no one knew who the lucky man had been. None of the young men who had been flirting with her stepped forward and confessed to being the father, which is what usually happened in these cases. For her part, Susanna steadfastly refused to point him out, not even to her mother.

A healthy baby was born and christened Katerina, Katie for short. Before long she was crawling around on the floor inside the cottage where Susanna lived with her mother and father and, later, playing games with the other children outside in the street. But the innocence of little Katie's childhood was blighted when it became obvious that instead of the frizzy little curls of her playmates, the baby fluff on her head was growing into long silken straight black hair.

Heads began to wag. The father was a White man, most probably from one of the families in the village that Susanna had worked for. There was nothing she could do but watch helplessly as her shame slowly crowned the head of her innocent little daughter. Shortly after Katie's birth Susanna had been forced by her parents into a marriage with Jaap September. 'Your daughter needs a father,' she was told 'and you need a husband.' Susanna submitted, but as it turned out the marriage – which was childless – did not protect the little girl from what life had in store for her. Inevitably the day came when she burst into the house crying and buried her face in her mother's skirts. One of her playmates had turned on her spitefully in a game:

'You don't belong here. Go look for your daddy in the village.'

When that happened a second time, and a third, and a fourth, Susanna could no longer endure little Katie's distress. She sat her down on the bed and tried to explain to her that God had made her hair straight to remind her mother of a big sin she had committed, a sin she would tell Katie all about when she was big enough to understand. Then, stifling her own tears, she went and fetched a pair of scissors and cropped Katie's hair right down to the scalp and after that tied the first doek on the naked little head. She also made her promise that, for her mother's sake, she would from then on always wear a doek, or a hat on Sundays, when she went out of the house. The little girl made the promise. After that day, with a few exceptions, no one in the village or the location saw Katie Koopman's hair again. For a few years Susanna made a regular practice of cropping her daughter's hair, but Katie became curious to see what she would look like with a full head of hair and after much cajoling and pleading Susanna abandoned the scissors. Mother and daughter watched with guilty delight as the stubble on the young head grew longer and longer.

The only person, other than her mother and father, to see the beauty that was hidden under that doek was Jannie Koopman, the man Katie married. He saw it and loved it late at night when Katie felt safe from unexpected visitors and untied the doek. At first they were just tantalisingly brief glimpses because Katie was always anxious to blow out the candle just in case someone was peeping in through the threadbare curtains. This of course only fueled Jannie's passion and eventually drove him to make shutters for all the windows so that Katie would feel safe from prying eyes. The doek would come off and there lay the thick jet-black braid, coiled like a sleeping snake at the back of her head.

When Katie took out the hair clip that held her hair in place, it dropped all the way down to her waist. Jannie loved to play with it, running the soft, silken length of it through his hands, calling it his Black Mamba. When he did this Katie closed her eyes and laughed with shy delight. But Jannie's love was a guilty love. Katie had told him the story of her mother's sin and God's punishment. Caressing that braid of hair he couldn't help thinking that maybe it was just such a snake that had made Eve tempt Adam to sin in the Garden of Eden. But he kept these thoughts from Katie.

Marie was born in the fourth year of their marriage. The months leading up to her birth were an anxious time for the young couple, but as it turned out their fears were groundless. A healthy baby was born and it soon became obvious that she had not been marked by her grandmother's sin. Jannie lived long enough to see his daughter grow up into a beautiful and strong-willed young girl who shared his love of that cascade of shining hair that came spilling out at night when Katie took off her doek. But Marie's was not a guilty love. As she grew, she began to resent the secret and the burden of shame that was insidiously passed on to her. How could something so beautiful be God's punishment? And why Katie? She hadn't done anything wrong. God should have put the straight hair on Susanna's head.

Reinforcing these questions was also an awareness in the young girl that things were changing, that the ways and judgments of the old people were being challenged. Once or twice she had tried to summon up enough courage to confront her mother with these thoughts and questions, but the shadow of fear that passed over Katie's face when she did this, always defeated her. Like her father, she did not have the heart to disturb the quiet of her mother's life. The little flame of rebellion in Marie's heart was snuffed out finally with her marriage to Apools. He was a firm believer in the ways and judgments of the old people. When Marie shared the family secret with him just before their marriage he had had no hesitation in endorsing the justice of God's punishment. Pumping that organ on Sunday for Mrs de Bruyn had inflated his soul with fear of the Almighty.

The last initiate into the circle of secrecy was Marie's lammetjie – little Yolanda. There had been a few anxious moments leading up to her birth as well, but when she arrived it was obvious that like her mother she had escaped God's wrath. By then time had transformed the black snake curled up under her grandmother's doek into a rope of the purest silver. Like her grandfather before her, the moment Yolanda always waited for was when Katie undid the plait and shook her head gently from side to side, her hair floating around like moonlight in the tumbling waters of the Gatsrivier when it came down in flood.

Yolanda's special time for loving it was Sunday afternoon when she and her mother would stroll over to Katie's house to help her bath and to wash and dry her hair. At first Yolanda was too young to do anything except sit and watch and get in the way. But a day came, when after much pestering her mother finally handed her the hairbrush and from then on it became her responsibility and delight to look after Ouma's hair. While she did this the two older women would relax into long lazy sessions of gossip and memories, Katie entertaining them with stories of the old days and Marie keeping her mother up to date with all that was going on in the location. Katie was becoming frail, and the walk to the church on Sundays was all that she could now manage.

One Sunday, having run out of good gossip, Marie mentioned, almost as an afterthought, that big things were going on in the outside world: Old De Klerk was going to let the even older Old Mandela out of jail.

'And when he does that Mommy God alone knows what all is going to happen in the country.'

Marie brought other items of news like this one about things that were happening up in the Transvaal where the Whites and the Blacks were busy killing each other. In this she reflected what was happening in the location generally. From total indifference or sceptical head-shaking people were starting to listen more care-fully to what the wireless was saying about a 'New South Africa'. The loud and angry voices of politicians trying to inflate their small roles in the epic drama that was taking place could be heard everywhere. Big words that formerly could only be found in the dictionary in the School Principal's office – 'Democracy', 'Negotiations', 'Truth and Reconciliation' – were now bandied about in the houses and streets of the location. Marie dutifully carried them to those Sunday afternoon sessions with Katie and tried to explain to her and understand for herself what they meant. Standing quietly behind her grandmother and running the hairbrush through her long silver hair, Yolanda saw in her mother's face and heard in her voice a mixture of excitement and anxiety, nervous little laughs followed by frowns and head-shaking that always ended with: 'I don't know where it's all going to lead to.'

The reason for Marie's uncertainty about the future was a fundamental difference of opinion between herself and her husband on the subject of the 'New South Africa'. Apools's routine as Church Caretaker included arriving on Sundays a good hour before the congregation so that he could help Mrs de Bruyn prepare everything for the service. This meant laying out the hymn books, putting up the numbers of the hymns that were to be sung in that service, and then placing on either side of the pulpit the two vases of flowers that Mrs de Bruyn had carefully arranged. After retiring to the little pump cubicle next to the organ to wait for the start of the service, Mrs de Bruyn had taken it upon herself to use the time to prepare Apools for the elections which were now only a few weeks away. And Apools, who knew that his job depended totally on her goodwill, listened carefully to everything she had to say.

According to Mrs de Bruyn the first thing he had to understand was that all this talk about 'Freedom' and 'Change' was just a lot of nonsense. Everybody already had as much freedom as they needed and nothing was going to change. Secondly, Mr de Klerk was a traitor and that old Mandela was only interested in the Blacks. They were the ones who were going to get rich. The only people who really cared about the Coloureds were the Afrikaners.

'Go speak to your people Apools. Tell them not to listen to all the nonsense the Black politicians are talking.'

When Apools dutifully did so there were always a few, made cynical and bitter by years of hardship, who would nod their heads in agreement. As one of them put it:

'We weren't white enough in the old South Africa and we won't be black enough in the new one.'

Among those he could not convince, however, was his wife Marie. At first, like the good wife she was, she had listened respectfully as he repeated the gospel of doubt that Mrs de Bruyn had instilled into his soul. But within her, her long-dormant instincts had stirred into life and were telling her that the time had come for change and a future that would give her lammetjie opportunities that she herself had never had. These instincts eventually forced her out of her silence. First there were just simple questions, then timid disagreement, until finally she was arguing head on with a furious Apools.

Where Apools was frightened of losing the little they had, Marie wanted more. Where Apools had decided to please Mrs de Bruyn and vote for Boetie Greyling, the retired Police Sergeant who owned the Trading Store, Marie was determined to put her cross next to the name of Mr Vyvers, the Coloured School Principal. It was heavy going in their little house in that last week before polling day. In most situations Apools Olifant was a weak man but in the privacy of his home he had always laid down the law and Marie in turn had always been ready with an obedient 'Yes Apools'. Now, for the first time, she shook her head and said 'No'. What is more, she was determined that, come hell or high water in the Gatsrivier, her mother would be there next to her in the queue on Polling Day and that Katie would also put her cross next to Mr Vyver's name.

Marie went to work on her mother with a passion every bit the equal of that which Mrs de Bruyn brought to bear on the hapless Apools. Katie listened quietly as Marie intoned the liberation litany of Freedom, Equality and Democracy and explained over and over again what was going to happen and where she must put her mark on the ballot paper. Katie could read and write and her eyesight was still quite good. When Marie asked at the end of those sessions 'Does Ma understand?' there was always the same quiet 'Yes my child' in reply. But secretly Marie despaired at the thought of what her her mother might do all alone in the voting booth.

On the afternoon before the election Marie and Yolanda were back in the shuttered house to give Katie a bath and wash her hair. During the hair-combing, Marie announced that because the next day was going to be such an important one in their lives, they would all dress in their best Sunday clothes. After cooking up a meal for Katie and wrapping it up in a blanket to stay warm until she felt hungry, Marie went home with Yolanda to do the same for themselves and Apools when he came home from work.

Despite the big day that was coming, the candles and lamps of the location did not burn late into the night. A hot dry berg wind had blown all day, spinning the windmills giddily and stirring up clouds of dust in the streets. Men working out in the fields tied handkerchiefs to cover their noses and mouths and even the shortest walk outdoors left you with the taste of the Karoo on your tongue. At the end of the day there was no energy left for anything except to wash your swollen red eyes, eat your supper and go to bed. Even Marie and Apools finally declared a truce in their argument about the election and what the New South Africa was going to mean to them. There were many more real and immediate issues to stare at in the dark as they lay side by side in bed: Yolanda needed new shoes, Apools a new pair of khaki trousers, and then there was the one hundred rand he was going to have to borrow from somewhere so that he could go up to Colesburg for the funeral of his uncle, which meant they certainly wouldn't be able to get the two blankets she had hoped to buy the next winter … and what about twenty-five rand the municipality wanted from everyone to pay for the new seats in their outside toilets? Apools was already snoring when Marie finally curled into his back and closed her eyes.

Yolanda was still awake when her mother joined her father in their nightly chorus of snores, grunts and unintelligible mumbles. As usual she had turned on her side and feigned sleep when her parents started to undress, but when the candle was blown out she opened her eyes and looked at tomorrow, trying once again to understand what was going to be one of the most important days of her life. She could never make much sense of all that her mother had been saying to her grandmother. The important days she already knew were her birthday and Christmas Day and the day of the Sunday School picnic when they all climbed onto the village tractor and trailer and went out to Hans Conradie's farm to eat watermelon and cake and run races in the veld and then of course there was also the last day of school at the end of the year with its the school concert and prize giving. Tomorrow was obviously not going to be like one of those even though she would be wearing her best dress. There were also of course Wedding Days and Funeral Days when you also had to wear your best dress but those weren't really her days. They belonged to the person who was getting married or buried. Yolanda was searching for still other possibilities when she finally closed her eyes and fell asleep.

For Katie there was no sleep that night and the candle at her bedside burnt itself down to a little pool of wax. Hers was a long journey back in time, a journey that carried her through spasms of joy and sorrow as faces of the dead floated up out of the darkness, faces that sometimes stopped the flow of memories while she tried to remember their names, a journey that ended in the tear-stained face of a little girl with a doek on her head staring back at her in a mirror. At that point a surge of grief made her close her eyes and in the silence of that shuttered room she murmured aloud: 'Too long! It has been too long.'

The scorching wind of the previous day had died down when Yolanda opened the back door and looked out at the Big Day. The air was still hazy with dust from yesterday's wind and very still. Her mother had told her that it was going to be just like a Sunday – no school for the children and no work for the big people. Instead of going to church they would all go down to the village hall where the Police Sergeant would show them how to vote. And no, she couldn't vote even if her mother showed her how to do it. Why? Because she was still too small. But one day, when she was grown up ...

Standing there in her vest and broekies, Yolanda couldn't help thinking that a day as special as this one was supposed to be, deserved to be more than just another Sunday in the middle of the week. But as usual her mother was right. No doubt about it. The sounds and voices she heard were Sunday sounds and voices, slow and lazy with a lot of silence in between them. She stared at Khaki. He had sprung to his feet when she opened the door and stood there now in front of her straining at the end of the length of wire that tied him to the pepper tree, wagging his tail in the hope of a few scraps of bread or porridge. Even he knows, she thought. Any other weekday he would have been at the fence waiting for a chance to bark at anything that passed in the street.

Breakfast.

First the smell of methylated spirits and paraffin and then the forceful thump-thump-thump of her mother pumping the primus followed a few seconds later by a steady hiss as the little brass stove came to life. Yolanda put out mugs and plates and three spoons of rooibos tea in the teapot. Then the apricot jam. Her mother cut thick slices of bread. A very loud poep from under the blankets followed by a loud 'Ag nee wat Apools! Go do it outside!' from Marie and the man of the house got out of bed and made his way to the bucket toilet in the backyard. Yolanda's next chore was to take a basin of hot water, soap and towel outside for her father's wash. Khaki watched the comings and goings with bright black eyes and a tail that had settled down to a slow wag. Somewhere along the line there would surely be a scrap of something or the other.

Normally the walk to Katie's house was a leisurely affair with Marie using every opportunity that came along to stop and exchange pleasantries and gossip with friends. But this time her stride was quick and purposeful and Yolanda had to break into a little run once or twice to keep up with her. When she complained and asked her mother to slow down Marie reminded her that Katie took a long time to wash and get dressed and that the Voting People wouldn't wait for them all day. The only other time the little girl could remember her mother walking so fast was when little Hennie Carelse had come running to tell them that Katie had had a bad fall in her backyard.

This time Yolanda hung back in the yard to pat and talk to Lady while her mother went inside to help Katie wash and get dressed. Lady and Khaki had come from the same litter but temperamentally they were as different from each other as Katie was from her daughter. Where Khaki was invariably at the end of his chain, worrying about something in the street or the house, Lady was usually to be found sitting quietly in the old wooden box that served as her kennel. She was very fond of Yolanda and had come out with a wagging tail when she heard her voice in the distance. After a minute or so of patting and trying to catch Lady's tongue as she licked her hands, Yolanda suddenly realised she could not hear her mother fussing about in the kitchen. Where there should have been the rattle of pots and pans as Marie warmed up a kettle of water and the incessant flow of small talk, there was silence. Yolanda broke away from Lady, jumped up the two steps to the kitchen door and looked inside. What she saw would become one of the most enduring memories of her life and one she would always turn to whenever she needed courage to face one of life's challenges.

It was her mother who was sitting at the table this time, her elbows resting on it, her face buried in her hands, crying quietly. Standing next to her was Katie. There was no need for Marie to have rushed over the way she did, expecting to find her mother waiting patiently for her in her old pink dressing gown. Katie was already dressed and ready. Normally the sight of her mother crying would have sent Yolanda into a terrible panic, but this time her grandmother in her black dress with the pretty lace collar, the hat with flowers and the patent leather handbag held her full attention. What kept her staring, however, was the long, thick plait of silver hair that hung down unashamedly to her waist for the whole world to see and admire.

Katie laid a gentle hand on her daughter's head.

'There now my child. Wipe your eyes and let us go vote. It's going to be alright. You'll see. Everything will be alright.'

At the sound of the car Marie had arranged to give them a ride to the community hall, Katie turned to Yolanda:

'Little darling, go tell Mr Vyvers your Ouma says thank-you but because it is such a nice day, she wants to walk to the voting place.'

A little later Katie Koopman, with her daughter and grand-daughter on either side, stepped out into the broad corrugated road that led into the village. There were a few other people headed in the same direction and one by one they drifted over and fell in behind the three women. No one remarked on the fact that Katie had let her hair down but all were eager to agree that it was indeed a very nice day for voting and a fitting end to what had been a good year. Most of the houses in the location had pumpkins on their roofs and potatoes in the kitchen. But the real harvest of that day was in the hearts of the people shuffling forward to put their mark on a piece of paper. Katie Koopman had given them their first lesson in the meaning of the Freedom they had waited for so long.

BOOITJIE BARENDS

How can it all go just like that, he thought, just disappear without a trace like the heavy mist which at that moment was shrouding the tops of all the koppies surrounding the village. Booitjie was looking up at them, one hand steadying himself on a fence post the other one on his walking stick as he rested at the side of the road. All that loneliness and love and waiting ... gone! But of course the truth is they don't just vanish like that because God is waiting up in heaven and He knows all about what goes on down below here and He never forgets. Ja! It is just here on earth that all our stories are like the morning mist. And here on that earth, with legs that could now hardly carry him anymore, he was the only one left who knew Baas Gerrie Strydom's story — unless of course Miss Hannah de Bruyn had told it to someone just before she died. But that was very unlikely because who would want to tell that story to anyone here on earth ... and particularly Miss de Bruyn? That was one that should be told only to God on that day when you stood in front of Him and waited for His judgment. Shaking his head, Booitjie shuffled back slowly and painfully onto the road and continued on his way.

It was the news that the old Strydom house had been bought by one of the rich people from over the sea and that they were going to break it down and build a new one in its place that had started him living with Baas Gerrie's story once again and sent him hobbling off to see the old house for the last time before it also disappeared. His daughter had brought him the news together with his pension the day before, and that night, lying in bed, the memories had started to come back — maybe because that was how he had heard the story in the first place, lying awake in the dark while the old man, also wide awake in his bed on the other side of the room, stumbled into the telling of it.

But what frustrated Booitjie as he lay there with the memories of those nights coming back, and prevented him from getting any sleep at all that night, was that they came back to him all muddled and mixed up. The more he tried to sort out where and when this happened and that happened, the more it eluded him and the more impatient he became with himself and the greater became the obligation to get it right. After all, if he was the only one now who knew that story, wasn't it his duty to remember it properly? If the Day of Judgement was anything like what happened in the Court Room in Graaff-Reinet, might he not be called to give evidence? And so the idea came to him that maybe one last visit to the house would help him sort it out. If he stood in the room where, as a young man, he had shared those last nights of the old man's life, then surely he would remember it right.

In the years following Baas Gerrie's death Booitjie had of course passed the house many times and it had always pained him to see such a fine old building which held so many memories for him slowly start to age and show signs of neglect. The wonderful garden and orchard at the back had become overgrown with weeds, gutters had broken loose from the walls and roof because of the weight of leaves in them and were never repaired, as was the case also with the windows that naughty children had broken. When his knees finally made it too painful for him to walk long distances he had stopped seeing the house. In any case he knew what to expect now as he walked to it.

There were quite a few derelict old houses in the village and some of them had acquired a certain dignity, even a beauty as they crumbled away slowly into irreparable ruin. But when Booitjie finally reached Number 19 Immelman Street — to give the old Strydom house its official address — he realised that dignity had not softened the last days of Baas Gerrie's home. Standing there in front of it, Booitjie couldn't help thinking that it looked as if the mental anguish and pain of Gerhardus Strydom's last nights had spread to the very bricks and mortar of the house itself and that after his death it had matched the decay of his earthly remains with its own. The once neatly curtained windows were now blind unseeing holes in the walls with the scrap of a shutter hanging to the side of one of them, the once proud front door also hanging crookedly on one hinge with all of its green paint blistered away by the fierce Karoo sun and winds, while every wall had raw ulcerous patches where the plaster had fallen away.

It was not to that front door, however, that Booitjie Barends shuffled on his now badly swollen knees. Old habits die hard and so Booitjie made his way slowly around to the back door — there are certain things you don't forget even in your old age and for Booitjie one of them was that this had once been Baas Gerrie Strydom's house.

There were not many people left in the village to whom Gerhardus Daniel Lottering Strydom of the farm Verlorevlei was known personally, and the few elderly folk who remembered him did so mostly for the series of accidents and the bad luck that had blighted a happy and contented life in its prime. Up until then Gerrie Strydom was looked up to as an example of what a godfearing and hardworking man could achieve in the harsh and demanding world of the Karoo. He had taken over the struggling farm from his sick father in his late twenties and, during the next ten years, had transformed Verlorevlei into a showpiece of what progressive agricultural methods could achieve. This coupled with the fact that young Gerrie was a magnificent specimen of Karoo manhood — he stood six feet two inches in his socks — made him one of the most eligible young bachelors in the district. It therefore came as no surprise to anyone when Deborah de Bruyn, the elder of two very different but equally beautiful sisters, said 'Yes' without hesitation when he asked her to be his wife. Two years after their marriage Deborah gave birth to a little girl, Rebecca, who she and Gerrie proudly announced was going to be the first in a large family.

But that was not to be. A horse-riding accident when Deborah was three months pregnant with their next child resulted in a miscarriage and a damaged spine. A series of botched operations over the next few years left her permanently paralysed from the waist down, and her artistically gifted younger sister Hannah – who was studying art in Cape Town – put her career on hold and moved into Verlorevlei to look after the severely depressed Deborah and the infant Rebecca. By the time Deborah had worked her way out of her depression and achieved a bitter reconciliation with her fate, Hannah had made herself an indispensable member of the household. She stayed on and it looked for a time to the outside world as if some sort of peace had come back to Verlorevlei until Hannah was killed in a motorcar accident. Ten years later, Deborah fell victim to a flu epidemic that swept through the valley. A broken man, Gerrie eventually suffered two strokes which left him paralysed on his left side and with severely impaired speech.

This was the broken spirit and body that Gerrie's daughter – now Mrs Rebecca Kloppers – entrusted to the care of young Booitjie Barends. Because of his small size – five foot and one inch in his bare feet – most of the White people made the mistake of thinking that he could not do as good a day's work as any other man, and for this reason Booitjie was often hard up for work. The people of the location knew better, and when Mrs Rebecca Kloppers asked the Police Sergeant to recommend someone reliable to look after her father at night he had no hesitation in suggesting Booitjie. Mrs Kloppers had had her doubts as well, but she decided to trust the Police Sergeant's judgment and gave Booitjie the job. In laying out his responsibilities Mrs Kloppers had made it very clear to him that the job would not last long as the doctors had warned her that her father's system had been severely undermined by the two strokes and that the end could come at any moment.

'It is not a permanent position, Booitjie. My father is a very sick man and he hasn't got long to live, but we want these last days of his life to be as comfortable as possible. You must be very patient with him. The Oubaas was a man who used to do everything for himself so it is very hard for him now, specially as he can't even speak anymore and tell us what he wants. So it's a guessing game with him all the time and when you guess wrong he gets very cross. So your first job is to help him with everything ... eating, putting on his clothes in the morning, helping him to the lavatory and taking down his trousers and then wiping him clean afterwards. You must also work out a plan for a regular bath. Put all his dirty clothes in the laundry basket in the bathroom. I've got two girls from the location who will come in the mornings to take over from you. They will do the housework, his washing and feed him and so on. One thing you must know is that he was always a very fussy man about his appearance. So if you don't look after him properly you will quickly know all about it. Even though he can't speak he can make terrible noises when he is angry. But if he sees you are doing your job properly he won't give you too much trouble. The Oubaas is still on the farm at the moment but we will bring him to the house tomorrow so be ready to start work tomorrow night.'

After that conversation, which had taken place on the back stoep, Mrs Kloppers had led him to the bedroom, where he was to sleep with her father every night for the next eighteen months. What he remembered of that moment was standing, hat in hand, in the doorway while Mrs Kloppers gave instructions to the two 'girls from the location' — both of them mature women — who were putting linen on two beds: the large double one in the centre of the room and a single one up against a wall. There was also a wardrobe and dressing table, carpets on the floor and an armchair positioned next to the window so that anyone sitting in it could look out onto the street.

When Mrs Kloppers was finished with the women, she had

turned to Booitjie and beckoned him over to the wardrobe.
Suits, jackets and trousers were hanging on one side, shirts and
underclothing were neatly stacked in drawers on the other. Her
instructions to him were again very precise: every morning after he
had woken up, the old man was to be dressed in clean underwear,
suit, shirt and tie. When the girls arrived Booitjie would be free to
go back to the location until late afternoon when the women
would go home and he would take over again for the night.

Paused now, nearly fifty years later, once again hat in hand in
that same doorway, Booitjie could see no resemblance whatever in
the room in front of him to the one he remembered. It was as if
he had lifted the lid of the old man's coffin expecting to see him
lying there in the suit he had dressed him in the day that he died
and found only a few mouldy bones and ashes unto ashes. Years
of dust and leaves had blown in through the empty windows, a
swallow had built a next for a couple of seasons in one corner of
the ceiling, floor boards had collapsed and some vagrant had made
a fire in one corner which had left streaks of black soot on the
walls. It was almost too much for him. If his knees had been up to
it he would have turned around at that moment and left. All he
could do instead was to close his eyes and lean up against the wall
behind him.

Whoever had made that fire had used an old paint tin to sit on,
and it was to this that Booitjie now hobbled. Using his walking
stick he pushed it up against the wall and sat down on it. He did
so with difficulty but when he had sat down and stretched out his
legs the pain in his knees and his inner agitation began to subside.
He was able to look around and start his journey back in time to
the room he remembered. But to do that he first had to move the
furniture back in, the big stinkwood wardrobe and matching
dressing table against the wall opposite the big window, the little
washstand in the corner, the carpets on the floor, the arm chair at
the window and, last of all, the two beds: the old man's double
bed with its stinkwood headboard and matching bedside table and

the single iron bed with its sagging mattress on which Booitjie had slept.

Booitjie had taken on the job with very mixed feelings. On the one hand he urgently needed to earn some money as he was the only male in a household of dependent women: his eighty-five year old Ouma, his ailing mother and his simple-minded sister three years younger than himself. His Ouma's pension – their only income – barely managed to put enough food on the table for the four of them. But on the other hand there was the disturbing prospect of the man he would be looking after. There were strange stories about the formidable Baas Gerrie Strydom of Verlorevlei, stories that somehow linked him to the rusting shell of an old motorcar lying on its back at the bottom of Rubidge Kloof. It was said that a woman's voice calling for help could be heard some nights coming from that wreck at the bottom of the kloof.

Given all this it is not surprising that the first few weeks were a difficult time for both men. For Gerhardus Strydom there was the humiliation of having to endure a stranger's clumsy and nervous hands fumbling their way into the most private recesses of his body. Because of his helplessness they had to go where no pair of hands had ever been, other than his own and his mother's when he was an infant. What made it worse was that his daughter insisted on supervising the first few times that Booitjie dressed and undressed her father. Gerrie had tried his best to get rid of her by using language that only errant farm labourers had ever heard from his mouth. It didn't work however because that mouth and the clumsy tongue inside it could no longer shape the necessary consonants and vowels. Rebecca knew her father well enough to know what he was trying so say but she stood her ground and directed Booitjie's trembling hands as he struggled to pull up underpants, put legs into trousers and get arms into sleeves. The last vestige of pride left in the old man made him hold back his tears until the evening when he was tucked away in bed and Booitjie had blown out the candles.

The most daunting of all the challenges that Booitjie faced during those first few weeks was Baas Gerrie's weekly bath. The problem was quite simply Baas Gerrie's size. Gerhardus Strydom had been a big and powerful man and, although his muscles had turned to flab as a result of the stroke, he hadn't as yet lost much weight. Booitjie, as his nickname indicated, was at the other extreme of the scale. Getting Gerrie Strydom to and then into the bath was a desperate business, with the old man roaring at the top of his stroke-impaired voice while he and Booitjie floundered around in the bathroom like two very drunk men supporting each other. The situation was made even more desperate for Booitjie on one occasion when the old man slipped on the wet floor and went crashing down. No bones were broken that time but Booitjie realised that they might not be so lucky if it happened again.

The solution, finally, was a very simple one: Baas Gerrie Strydom was going to get his bath location style. With the consent of Mrs Kloppers, a large zinc bath, like the one in which the household laundry was washed once a week, was bought and installed in the bathroom. All the old man had to do was to step into this carefully and then hold on to the towel rack while Booitjie soaped and sponged him down, standing on a little wooden box to reach the top of his head. The old man's relief and gratitude were obvious. The first of those standing-baths marked the beginning of the bond of mutual trust that came to characterise his relationship with Booitjie.

It also left Booitjie with one of the most extraordinary images any Coloured man had of his 'master', standing there naked, facing the wall with his arms stretched out as he held on to the towel rack. It took the younger man only a few seconds to realise where he had seen that massive white presence before: it was the old bluegum tree in front of the village trading store when it had shed its bark in spring, revealing a surface as astonishingly smooth and white and living as the one that glowed in front of Booitjie in the bathroom. The two varicose-veined ankles and calves standing in the water seemed as rooted to the earth as the old tree which in Booitjie's lifetime alone — it had been there long before him — had survived no fewer than five lightning strikes. Two powerful sets of calf muscles ballooned out into the heavy thighs, the sagging buttocks and the huge barrel of a body.

The bath always started with a dripping sponge on the top of the old man's head. The rhythm of squeezing it and watching the water trickle down the broad back and chest never failed to give Booitjie a keen pleasure that the old man himself began to share. Booitjie fancifully thought of it as Baas Gerrie's personal passing shower and, just as the air outside the Trading Store was filled with the scent of eucalyptus after the tree had received its share of a thunderstorm, so did the bathroom fill with the scent of Lifebuoy soap as Booitjie lathered and then rinsed down the massive body.

In about three months Gerrie Strydom and Booitjie Barends had sorted out their difficulties and misunderstandings and worked out a routine that for the most part carried them safely through the night. There were of course always interruptions such as the old man needing to go to the lavatory — right up to his last day he refused to use a bed pan — or wanting a drink of water and even, one night, making Booitjie fetch a family album of photographs and page through it. And all the time there were the old man's mumbles and mutterings. Mrs Kloppers had told Booitjie to ignore these sounds which she said were like the noises that little babies make before they can talk. The only sound he was to pay attention to was the ringing of the little bell that she had placed on her father's bedside table. The old man could still manage to reach out and shake it.

It was in the fourth month of their nights together that Booitjie discovered that the old man's mutterings and mumbles were not quite as meaningless and incomprehensible as Mrs Kloppers had said. It had started very simply at the end of another standing-bath when the old man had made the little mumble he used to make when it was over and which Booitjie had come to accept as a token of gratitude. He always responded to it with a cheerful 'That's okay Oubaas', but on this occasion, because he was now feeling very comfortable with the Oubaas, he added a few extra words: 'Thunder clouds in the sky when I walked over this afternoon. I think we might get a few showers tonight.' This elicited another mumble from the old man.

Booitjie left it at that as he got Gerrie Strydom into his pyjamas and then into bed. After that he emptied the bath water, put the underclothing, socks and shirt in the wash basket and hung up the jacket and trousers. It was while he was sitting in the kitchen eating the plate of food that 'the girls' had laid out for him that he realised that that last mumble from the old man had been a meaningful response to what he, Booitjie, had said about the possibility of rain. He could recall the mumble very clearly – *letushopesobooitjie* – and after listening to its echo in his mind a couple of times he decided that the old man had said 'Let us hope so Booitjie'. A spoonful of beans and rice remained suspended midway between his open mouth and the plate on the table as he realised that he and the old man had talked to each other. And what is more, he had used Booitjie's name.

Booitjie did not have to wait long for confirmation. It did rain that night. After a spell of violent thunder and lighting that flashed incandescent images of the room into the wide awake eyes of the two men, the rain came down on the corrugated iron roof in a five-minute drum roll that left images in Booitjie's mind of flooded location roads and, in Gerrie Strydom's, of a churn of muddy water in the normally dry spruit below the Verlorevlei homestead. In the silence that followed the downpour a loud mumble – *wonderfulrain* – came from the double bed and Booitjie had no trouble understanding what it meant.

Over the course of the next few months Booitjie slowly mastered the old man's vocabulary of throaty grunts and mumbles to the point where the two of them could have quite a sustained conversation. The subject matter was always very simple and mostly concerned the weather, the household routine and occasionally a bit of innocent gossip that Booitjie had picked up at the Trading Store. Booitjie had tried to tell Mrs Kloppers what was happening but unfortunately chose a moment when she was both in a hurry and very angry – she was on her way to Graaff-Reinet where her youngest son was to appear in court on a charge of drunk driving. She dismissed Booitjie's tentative approach with a 'No, not now. Talk to me next time.' Booitjie never did.

The relationship between the two men moved to a new level on the night that Booitjie was awakened, not for the first time, by the ringing of the bell. He scrambled out of bed and hurriedly lit a candle thinking that something was wrong. He found the old man sitting calmly on the side of his bed.

'Lavatory Oubaas?'

Gerrie shook his head.

diningroom

Their destination in that room turned out to be the large ornate sideboard with beveled mirrors that stood commandingly against one wall. Booitjie was made to pull out the bottom drawer and take out of it two large leatherbound family photograph albums. That done they shuffled back to bedroom where he helped the old man to get back into his double bed and propped him up in a sitting position with pillows against the headboard and the albums in his lap. Booitjie was made to stand next to the bed and turn the pages of one of the albums.

With grunts and a few taps of a gnarled forefinger, which Booitjie took to mean 'Yes, I remember' Gerhardus Strydom acknowledged the photographs of long-dead forebears and relatives, most of them taken with the Verlorevlei farmhouse in the background. Then Gerrie and his dead sister Alida began to dominate the pages – first as babies, then toddlers, then teenagers in smart school uniforms and, eventually, as a young man and young woman with friends, rackets in hand on the farm tennis court or mounted on horses or in swimming costumes at the farm

dam – images that accurately reflected their carefree existence
during those early years of their lives. After a few pages there was
a photograph of two beautiful young women who had not yet
appeared in the album. Booitjie turned the pages more slowly, the
old man lingering over every image of the two De Bruyn sisters.
As unused as Booitjie was to studying photographs, he was
immediately struck by how different the two young women
looked.

Though he would have been hard pressed to put it into words,
Booitjie was as struck by the extrovert physical radiance of
Deborah de Bruyn as he was by the quiet introversion of Hannah.
It was there in body language and clothing as much as in their
beautiful faces. Conscious of how he was staring at the two young
women, he hastened to turn the page but was stopped by a
forceful No! from the old man. He looked up in time to see a
single tear run down Gerrie Strydom's cheek. He muttered the two
names *deborahhannah*, then closed his eyes and signaled to Booitjie to
take the albums away. They went back into the bottom drawer of
the sideboard.

Booitjie could not get that solitary tear out of his mind. He
had never seen a White man cry before and it made him very
nervous. For the next few nights he waited for a sequel to that
session with the albums but it did not come. Several weeks later,
however, the bell rang again in the dark. This time the candlelight
revealed the old man lying still in his bed. He looked expectantly
at Booitjie and patted the blankets over his lap. Booitjie knew
immediately what he wanted. He fetched the albums from the
bottom drawer of the sideboard. When he placed the first one in
Gerrie's lap it fell open at the page where they had stopped the last
time. This time Booitjie made no move to turn the page until he
received a signal to do so.

The snapshots on the following pages, all of them held neatly
in place with little black corner stickers, were like windows
through which Booitjie caught intimate glimpses of another way

of life: braaivleises and parties on the front lawns of Verlorevlei, Christmas and birthday parties, and the life of young Gerrie himself – a gallery of pictures of the neatly blazered schoolboy outside the Volks Hoër School in Graaff-Reinet, the Stellenbosch University first-team rugby player and, later, the confident young farmer in the seat of his new tractor. Standing next to the bed as he turned the pages Booitjie studied the photographs with an intensity equal to that of the Oubaas himself.

The first of the albums climaxed on its last crowded pages with wedding photographs of Deborah on the arm of a very serious Gerhardus Daniel Lottering Strydom in front of the village church, both of them speckled with confetti. Hannah, standing behind her sister, was barely visible. The second album started off with more photographs of what Booitjie had come to think of as 'the Oubaas's happiness'. A little baby appeared in the arms of a very proud mother, its growth into toddler and then little girl chronicled on the pages that followed. They ended abruptly with a photograph that occupied a page all to itself: an image of Hannah looking thoughtfully at the camera. There were a lot of empty pages left in the second album. The camera had obviously been put away and not used again.

Those late candlelit hours when the rest of the village was fast asleep and the two family snapshot albums were on the old man's lap created a deep bond between the two men. Nothing was said apart from an occasional grunt or mumble when a gnarled and trembling hand stretched out to tap a photograph and murmur a name as they studied the pages in silence. But one night, after Booitjie had put away the albums and blown out the candle and was lying wide awake in his bed wondering who the beautiful Coloured maid was who had appeared briefly in an early photo- graph holding the baby and was never seen again, the old man broke the silence with a word that Booitjie recognised immediately as Hannah. It was followed by a long silence until Booitjie, sensing that the old man was waiting for something from him, also spoke

into the darkness: 'I hear you Oubaas.' Just a short pause this time
and the old man continued:

hannahdebruyn — sheshouldneverhavecome

The seconds of heavy expectant silence in the room stretched
into minutes while Booitjie waited for the Oubaas to say something
more but nothing was forthcoming. Eventually Booitjie fell asleep.

The next night the Oubaas did not ask for the albums. In fact it
looked to Booitjie as if he were impatient for the day to end and
the candles to be blown out. When Booitjie had finally settled
down for the night on the tired springs of his metal bed, the
old man wasted no time, mumbling into the darkness as if the
previous evening had continued uninterrupted.

jaiwashappybooitjie ...

... and then a sound that could have been laughter ...

... *happy ... gerhardusdaniellotteringstrydom ... marriedtodeborah ...
deborahsusannadebruyn ... everythingIwanted ... verlorevlei ... beautiful-
deborah ... andme ... strong ... healthy ...*

Slurring out sentences as crooked and eroded as a Karoo donga,
Gerrie Strydom re-lived the six happiest years of his life. In what
was to become an established pattern, Booitjie listened respectfully, gaining only the general drift of what the old man was
telling him. In the long silence that settled in after the Oubaas fell
asleep again, Booitjie would work out that night's episode from his
rough understanding of what had been said and the many pictures
in the photo album. The first of these montages was 'the wedding
of the year' which had launched those six years of unalloyed
happiness. There had been over a hundred laughing, well-wishing
friends and relatives on the lawns and stoep of Verlorevlei with
just such a grand party also for Booitjie's people — the farm
labourers and the domestic servants — at the back of the house.
At the end of the braaivleis there on the lawns all the talking and
laughing was hushed when the volk came around from their party
to sing hymns and to wish young Baas Gerrie and his beautiful
bride a long and happy life. Because they all loved him you see. He

was a good master, working shoulder to shoulder with the labourers from sunrise to sunset. Ja! Together they had made Verlorevlei one of the most successful farms in the district. And as if all of that wasn't enough, in the second year of his marriage the Almighty blessed him and Deborah with a beautiful daughter. She was christened Rebecca de Bruyn Strydom — she had grown up into the intimidating Mrs Kloppers that Booitjie had to deal with. Booitjie saw plenty of pictures of her as a little baby in the picture album, in her mother's arms, in Baas Gerrie's arms and, in one snapshot, in the arms of that beautiful young Coloured maid.

Each night's mumblings required a Herculean effort on the old man's part, an effort that sapped him of his steadily diminishing strength. The growing intimacy between them frightened Booitjie who realised that he was being made privy to secrets that Baas Gerrie had never shared with anyone else. But as Booitjie's journey into that private world went deeper, fascination slowly overcame fear. He was present as a small brown doppelganger not just at the parties of Verlorevlei but deep in the bedrooms of the Strydom family eavesdropping on their most personal secrets.

At first it looked as if Booitjie's nightly adventure might end with the birth of little Rebecca because the old man lapsed thereafter into silence. The quietness that descended was broken only by the noises of their usual routine and Booitjie's occasional offerings of village gossip. But one night after Booitjie had blown out the candle and was yawning himself into sleep, the old man picked up the thread of his story once again:

areyouawakebooitjie

'Ja Oubaas.'

thatwashappinesswasntit

'Ja Oubaas ... that was now really happiness ... but is there no more pictures Oubaas?'

nomorepicturesbooitjiebecausehappinessended

It soon became clear to Booitjie that Baas Gerrie was entering a darker period of his life.

shewasexpecting — threemonths — oursecondchild — veryfondofhorseriding — ibeggedhertostop — waituntilbabywasborn — wouldn'tlisten — oneday . . .

It all started innocently enough. One day when Gerrie was in Graaff-Reinet Deborah got Ou Sarel — an elderly family servant who looked after the garden and the stables — to saddle up Sokkies for a ride in the veld. In doing this she broke a promise to her husband that, because of her condition, she would never go out riding if he wasn't there to join her. As Deborah told the story later she had only intended a short ride and had specifically asked for Sokkies because that animal was the oldest and safest of their four horses. Not too old, however, not to be startled when a six-foot Rinkhals reared up suddenly in front of her. Debora was equally unprepared and was thrown violently to the ground. She lay there with a broken hip for a couple of hours until a frantic Gerrie finally found her. He was too late to save the life of what would have been their second child. A botched operation put Deborah in a wheelchair for the rest of her life and ended all hope of another child. The old man ended this episode of his story with one strangled phrase which he turned into a mantra of despair, intoning it in the darkness: *ourhappinesslost . . . ourhappinesslost . . . lost . . . . . .* his voice eventually trailing away into silence.

He had forced out his story in chopped-up phrases and half sentences interrupted by long pauses as he struggled with his emotions, and the bedroom window was already filling with the first light of a new day when he finally ended. Lying in his bed, a wide-awake Booitjie needed all his ingenuity to assemble the pieces into a coherent narrative and when he had done that, when he had the whole of it in his mind, he marveled once again at how different the Oubaas's world had been to his own. The only personal point of reference he had was the time when he had tried to ride Blaauberg — Jacob van Staden's donkey — and had been thrown to the ground. Bruises yes, but no broken bones. He sat up in bed and looked across the room at the big double bed. There wasn't enough light as yet to see the other man.

'Is the Oubaas alright?'

He received no answer. At first Booitjie thought that the old man had fallen asleep, but then it dawned on him that something much more serious might have happened. He got out of bed and lit the candle. The eyes were indeed closed, but two gnarled and trembling hands on the eiderdown suggested that Gerrie was still very much alive.

'Is the Oubaas alright?'

This time he got an answer.

gosleepbooitjie — gosleep

In the weeks that followed, Gerrie Strydom once again lapsed into a heavy brooding silence. On his side Booitjie was left to puzzle over the questions the mumbled story had left him with. Was there more to it than that terrible fall that put Deborah Strydom in a wheelchair for the rest of her life? Everybody knew that she lived for many years after that. And what about the other sister who died so young when she crashed her car? Booitjie puzzled over these and many other questions when a sudden deterioration in the Oubaas's condition produced a distracting flurry of activity in the house. It had happened during the day shift, the old man thrashing around in his bed and whimpering like an injured dog while the girls from the location watched helplessly. When Booitjie arrived in the late afternoon the doctor's car was parked in front of the house. Booitjie found the girls in the second bedroom making up two beds because, as they told him in whispers, Mrs Kloppers and her ten-year-old son were going to sleep over as the end was now very near.

When Rebecca Kloppers saw Booitjie standing hat in hand in the doorway of the room he and her father had shared these many months, she beckoned him in and left the room with the doctor and her son. Approaching on tip toe Booitjie found it very easy to believe that the end was near. He patted the gnarled old hand, unable to restrain a whispered 'Haai shame Oubaas!'

Suddenly the old eyes opened and looked at Booitjie. There was a feeble mumble:

tellmewhentheyregone

Booitjie patted the gnarled old hand tentatively.

'I will Oubaas. Sleep now.'

Booitjie had learned much earlier to read the old man's signs of irritation when his daughter appeared at his bedside. With the new order in the household and Gerrie Strydom's weakened condition, he gave up all hope of a continuation of the story. But one night, after Mrs Kloppers had returned to the farm, the old man stopped Booitjie just as he was on the point of blowing out the candle and asked him to fetch the photo albums. This time they began at the last picture in the second album. Hannah de Bruyn stared enigmatically up at them from the old man's lap. The old man nodded his head silently before waving the book away. He sank back on his pillows and closed his eyes.

hannahdebruyn ... hannah ... hannah ...

Because it was the last thing he expected from the Oubaas it took Booitjie a long time to identify the emotions that had forced the old man's voice into a barely audible whisper, almost choking it into silence. They were fear and shame.

For Hannah de Bruyn those many years ago, the few weeks that she had anticipated spending at Verlorevlei comforting her sister and helping with the little Rebecca had stretched into months as Deborah spiraled in and out of a black depression that made her almost unrecognisable to her distraught husband. Again and again Hannah would be awoken at night to listen to Deborah's diatribes against her fate, her husband, herself. And always her wish to end it all, to be done with the pain, the uselessness, the anger.

itwas ... terrible ... terriblebooitjie ... hell ... livinginhell ... verlorevlei-wasahouseofsorrow ... oneday ... beautifulspringday ... icarriedher ... likeadeadlammetjie ... myarms ... frombedroomtothestoep ... sunshine ... flowersinthegarden ... theflowers ... sheplanted ... nothing ... nosmile ... nohappiness ... shesaid ... youshotsokkies ... nowshootmegerrie ... getyour-gunandshootme ...

And then a terrified Booitjie received the first of the old man's confessions: he would have done it. As true as there is a God in heaven he would have taken his revolver and shot Deborah and then put the barrel in his mouth and pulled the trigger. Why didn't he, because he was ready to do it? Rebecca, his little daughter who at that moment was playing with Hannah on the lawn in front of them. It was the sight and sound of their laughter that had made Deborah wish for death. But in turn, in the strange way that these things worked, it was the sight and sound of his daughter, the thought of her young life that had already been so bruised by what had happened to her mother, that made Gerrie shake his head and put his hand on his wife's shoulder.

no ... nomydarling ... no ... ibegyou ... don'teveraskmethatagain

Gerrie Strydom was a man who had always prided himself on having his emotional life firmly under control. The occasions when he spoke about his deepest feelings to someone else were few and far between, and even then the recipient of those rare confidences got no more than a hint of what really went on inside the heart and mind of this big and powerful man. His wife was no exception. On the night before their wedding when they were sitting up late on the stoep discussing the honeymoon they had planned down in Mosselbaai, Deborah had turned to him and half jokingly said that she didn't really know who the man was that she was going to marry the next day. Young Gerrie thought it was a joke and laughingly told her that she would find out soon enough. She never did. What she had really known about him sitting there on the stoep that night was still all she knew about him on that day seven years later when she mounted Sokkies intending to go for just a short ride in the veld.

Gerrie's proud emotional independence was severely tested and finally broken by what happened on that ride. The final blow came when he found himself imagining his wife's death and his own suicide. Had that despairing scenario come only once, it might have been possible for him to forget he had ever considered it, but when in the course of the next few months he found himself

thinking it a second and then a third and a fourth time it became
too much for him. He had to talk and unburden himself to
someone and that person turned out to be Hannah. It happened
one evening when the two of them were brooding in front of the
remains of a fire – it was late May and the nights were already
very cold. Their conversation had started off in a very desultory
fashion, both of them taking turns to recount trivial incidents in
their day and very obviously avoiding the one subject that was
uppermost in their minds – Deborah and her condition. It had
been one of her bad days when, goaded by pain, both mental and
physical, she had lashed out at everybody, her husband in
particular. The only person she had spared was her sister who
was now the only person in her life that she trusted.

Watching her sister reduce the innocent Gerrie to dumb misery
– he never said a word to defend himself from Deborah's cruel
and unjust accusations – was almost more than Hannah could
endure. Once or twice she had been on the point of intervening
but had stopped herself in time, realising that she would only add
another complication to an already impossible situation. Gerrie
was not aware of the bond that his wife was unwittingly forging
between him and the beautiful young woman sitting opposite him.
Locked away in his despair he had in fact taken Hannah for
granted until that moment in front of the fireplace. Looking at
her now it suddenly dawned on him just how much of the time
and energy of her young life she was sacrificing to look after her
sister and little Rebecca. What everyone had initially assumed was
going to be a visit of a few weeks, had already stretched into
almost a year. The thought of what it would be like without
Hannah made him close his eyes and hold out a hand as if to wave
away that terrible prospect. A startled Hannah had sat upright in
her chair.

'What's the matter Gerrie? Are you alright?'

'Ja, ja! I'm okay.'

'No you're not.'

'No truly I am ... it's just ...'

He paused.

'Just what Gerrie?'

'You.'

'What about me?'

'Haai Hannah. I don't think I would have survived this time if you hadn't been here.'

'What do you mean?'

'You haven't just helped Deborah ...' He put a hand on his chest.

'... me as well. You've also been my lifesaver ... because without you ...'

This was a moment that Hannah had long been waiting for but had been too frightened to initiate.

'Because without me what? Talk to me man. I know you are going through hell.'

Gerrie had sat back in his chair and stared at Hannah in silence for a few seconds, struck as never before by her dark brooding beauty. When he began to speak it was haltingly to begin with, because he had decided that he would tell her only how grateful he was for what she had done for his wife, his daughter and himself. She was a perfect example of what true Afrikaner womanhood was all about ... self-sacrifice ... his own mother had been cast in the same mould ... thanks to her his father had lived far longer than the doctors had ever predicted ... and so would Deborah thanks to her sister's self-sacrifice ... and himself also ... oh yes ... because he meant what he had said ... every word of it ... without her he didn't know what would have happened at Verlorevlei because ...

There was another long pause here but, this time, sensing that Gerrie was on the edge, Hannah had left it to him to carry on. He had. The thoughts and feelings he had been struggling in silence to suppress for the past few months took possession of him. He spoke very calmly and with methodical carefulness, choosing his words carefully. Another day like the one they had both just weathered and he would stand behind Deborah in her wheelchair, kiss the top of her head and then put the barrel of his revolver to the back of it and pull the trigger. He would pull up a chair, sit beside her there on the verandah, hold one of her limp and now useless hands in his, put the smoking barrel of his gun in his mouth with his other hand and pull the trigger once more. At the end of his confession he closed his eyes and waited.

Hannah had not uttered a word while he spoke. The silence in the room had turned as grey and cold as the ash in the fireplace when she finally stood up. Gerrie fully expected her to walk out of the room but, instead, with his eyes still closed, he felt her sit down beside him on the sofa. A gentle but firm hand on his shoulder made him open his eyes. She spoke as calmly and as carefully as he had:

'Stop now Gerrie. You've punished yourself enough. You aren't alone. Thoughts like that come to all of us. Yes! Don't think I haven't also had mine. We are only human.'

Forty years later the young Booitjie Barends had also listened in silence as old Gerhardus Strydom made that confession for the second time in his life. Booitjie had struggled to understand.

'Oubaas must go and sleep now. The girls will be here soon.'

He didn't have to wait long before the old man's snoring filled the room and he knew he could relax. Sleep however was out of the question for him and he was still wide awake when the two women entered the house through the back door. Normally he would have joined them for a few minutes of idle gossip but this time he ate his two slices of bread and jam and drank his coffee quietly and quickly before leaving. Without the distraction of their voices and the clatter of pots and pans, he was able to go over the latest instalment of the Oubaas's story as he walked back to the location.

Booitjie knew it was the truth ... so help him God, as they always said in the Magistrate's Court in Graaff-Reinet. But why had he told Booitjie? What was he supposed to do with it? Because what Booitjie also knew was that there was more to come. Should he tell the Oubaas to stop talking if he started again? Should he tell anyone about what the old man had told him? As it turned out his dilemma was resolved by the old man himself. When Booitjie took over from the location girls the next evening Gerrie Strydom was still too tired and drained of energy to do anything except eat a few spoonfuls of his supper and sink back onto his pillows. He was asleep even before Booitjie had blown out the candles. There was no talk between them that night and the next two nights were exactly the same. By the fourth night Booitjie's curiosity got the better of him and he tried to prod the Oubaas into life by repeating all the gossip he had heard and asking the old man questions. Eventually he came right out with it:

'Isn't the Oubaas going to finish his story?'

Gerrie did not even look at Booitjie. He simply closed his eyes and shook his head slowly.

So that was it. Booitjie would never know what had happened there on Verlorevlei although something obviously had. It came as a surprise to him when, taking over from the two women a few days later, he saw the photo albums on the old man's bedside table. He was on the point of asking why and how they were there but decided it would be wiser to wait for the old man to say something. Booitjie served him his supper and helped him to eat it. When he returned to the bedroom from the kitchen where he had scraped clean and washed the dishes, the old man nodded towards the albums.

comesitbooitjie

Booitjie hesitated.

bringachair

This time Booitjie obeyed. He brought a chair up to the bed and waited.

itwasntherfault! shewasinnocent! ididit thatsthegodstruth! iamtheguiltyone!

What was he talking about? Guilty of what? It was obviously something about Hannah de Bruyn because the old man turned back to the album that Gerrie had placed open on his lap, gently touching the young woman's picture while he continued talking. Bit by bit, the pieces of a dark and disturbing jigsaw puzzle were falling into place.

After that fateful night when Gerrie made his confession to Hannah, their relationship deepened steadily. In one of the cruel ironies of this story it looked almost as if the invalid sister was doing all she could to draw the other two together. In her private sessions with Hannah, the picture Deborah painted of Gerrie was a complete travesty of the man Hannah saw mute with misery in front of the fireplace in the evenings. The injustice of it affected her deeply and made her draw closer and closer to him. As if to make doubly certain that the inevitable would happen, Deborah then slowly began to turn on Hannah as well. It began with bitter remarks about how she was becoming little Rebecca's mother and that she, Deborah, no longer had any meaningful function in the house or Gerrie's life. These escalated imperceptibly to the point where she was saying that 'everyone' would be happy now if that horse-riding accident had had fatal consequences. Hitherto only Gerrie had been the target of these poison darts.

Hannah and Gerrie compared notes in the moments when they were together and most times these were late at night when Deborah had been sedated into sleep. Was it jealousy? Did she suspect that something was happening between them? Nonsense! It was only a friendship. A life-sustaining friendship but still only that. In this fashion they refused for some time to confront the truth about where their 'friendship' was headed. But even if they had it is doubtful if they could have stopped what was fated to happen. In yet another cruel irony it was Deborah's condition that helped their relationship to clear the final hurdle. The three had travelled down to Port Elizabeth, Deborah in an ambulance with a nurse followed by Gerrie and Hannah in a car. Deborah was to undergo another series of tests and treatment. She moved into a private ward in a clinic while Gerrie and Hannah stayed at a beachfront hotel.

Temporary escape from the oppressive atmosphere of Verlore-vlei gave Gerrie and Hannah a false and fatal sense of freedom. One night as they sat on the balcony of Hannah's room admiring the distant lights of the harbour and the ships at anchor in the bay, they stopped pretending. It was Hannah who took the initiative. She spoke softly:

'It's hell isn't it Gerrie.'

He of course knew what she meant.

'Ja, it's hell alright. I'm sorry ...'

She cut him off:

'No! Don't say anything. Just come with me. Please ...' She stood up and led him to her bedroom where they made love.

Gerrie was stricken with remorse and guilt.

'What have we done Hannetjie?'

Hannah's first response came in a quiet voice as they lay side by side on the bed:

'Made love Gerrie. That is what we've done.'

A pause followed and then in a voice that was fierce with passion and defiance:

'And I'm glad we did! Because I wanted it ... and so did you! What are you frightened of Gerrie? Judgment Day? The only hell we'll ever know is waiting for us there on Verlorevlei.'

She was right. With their desire for each other now released and rampant, life on Verlorevlei did become a torment unlike anything either of them had ever experienced. Their secret life as lovers was such a raw and humiliating experience that, coupled with Gerrie's guilt, their passion might well have died from sheer exhaustion had it been left alone to play itself out. One evening, however, Hannah returned from a day in Graaff-Reinet with the news that she was pregnant. This took their relationship to the edge. As far as Gerrie was concerned there was only one solution: young Dr Lubbe, his friend and tennis partner in the men's doubles at the farmer's social gatherings on weekends. Hannah was appalled. Abortion? It was *their* child! Not even fifteen minutes after telling her yet again how guilty he felt because he knew 'it was all his fault' he wanted to end the life of their child.

'No Gerrie! No! The only way you will kill this child is to kill me!'

This time it took a full hour of self-flagellation to find another solution. She must tell Deborah she wanted to get back to her studies, return to Cape Town, have the baby and then hand it over for adoption. There was a Dutch Reformed Church organisation to which the Strydom family and been generous contributors that placed unwanted babies in good Afrikaans foster homes. He would write to them and ...

Hannah was once again adamant.

'No Gerrie! This child is going to be born and I and no one else am going to be its mother!'

Scenes like this – progressively more bitter, angry and painful – played out during the following weeks. Hannah knew in her heart what the solution should be and she waited with growing desperation for Gerrie to see it, believing that if it came from him he would not be able to reject it. Gerrie on his side knew what it was but did everything possible to avoid confronting it until Hannah's patience finally ran out.

'Divorce, Gerrie. You must divorce Deborah.'

Gerrie closed his eyes and shook his head, waving a hand in front of him as if to erase the words that had been spoken. This had only fueled Hannah's anger and impatience.

'Yes! There's no other way. And stop shaking your head like that. You are the father of the child that is growing inside me. How many times have you told me that you love me? Prove it now Gerrie. Your life with Deborah is over for God's sake. It's dead!'

Gerrie stared down in disbelief at the violent, contorted face of the young woman he loved. Then, without another word, Gerrie turned his back on her, fetched his revolver and a handful of bullets from the safe in his office and stumbled out into the frost-sharp Sneeuberg night. He did not know where he was going. All he wanted was to get away from the house, sit down somewhere and put the barrel in his mouth and pull the trigger.

If it hadn't been for old Sarel, Gerrie might well have died that night. The family servant in his little cottage near the stables heard something moving around in the dark and, thinking that one of the horses might have broken out, went to investigate. He found Gerrie, blue-lipped and incapable of speech, stumbling around in his shirt sleeves like a drunk man. Dr Lubbe was summoned urgently, the servants having to wake Deborah to do this as the normally reliable Miss Hannah was nowhere to be found. Dr Lubbe said nothing about the revolver and bullets that Sarel discreetly gave him as he left the house. He held on to them for quite a long time before handing them back to Gerrie and then only after a long talk with him.

Two days later Dr Lubbe returned to the house, this time to examine and certify as dead the body of Hannah de Bruyn. A road gang had spotted her car at the bottom of a deep drop in Rubidge Kloof. It had gone straight over the edge on one of the sharp bends in the road. Her body was discovered half way up the steep incline. She had obviously survived the crash and was trying to reach the road, but one of her legs and an arm were broken and a shoulder dislocated. Hypothermia was given as the cause of her death, but the accident continued to puzzle. Where was she going in a such a hurry at that hour of the night? There was no luggage in the car! And the tyre tracks? They showed no sign of any attempt to swerve at the last moment but headed straight for the edge. These little questions were all the more puzzling because Hannah was the serious one of the two De Bruyn sisters. It was Deborah who had had the reputation of a reckless daredevil.

It was difficult for Booitjie to follow the last part of the Oubaas's story because the old man was overcome by his emotions, his body racked by violent sobbing. A terrified Booitjie did not know what to do. He tried to give the old man a drink of water but the glass was smashed out of his hands. Driven by desperation he finally tried to calm Gerrie by taking him in his

arms and making soothing sounds as he had seen location mothers
do when they comforted their crying babies. This had worked.
Like those infants his sobbing gradually subsided until at last
there was just an occasional whimper and convulsive intake of
breath as he lay cradled in the young man's arms. Looking down at
the tear-stained face on his chest Booitjie could hardly believe his
eyes. He had never even held a child like that leave alone a grown
man. A grown White man and an old one at that – in fact no less
a person than the formidable Gerhardus Daniel Lottering Strydom. No one would believe him. When the sobbing had subsided,
Booitjie lowered the old man onto his pillows and tucked him into
his blankets.

'Sleep now Oubaas.'

He carried the bedside candle over to his bed on the other side
of the room where he blew it out. There was still at least an hour
before the windows would fill with the grey light of a new day and
at least another hour after that before the girls from the location
would arrive to take over. Booitjie sat wide awake on his bed
through all of that time as he put together the last pieces of the
Oubaas's puzzle. Had he heard him right? Had he actually wanted
to fetch his revolver and shoot himself? Ja, he did. He said so
himself: Murder! And then what about Miss Hannah! Wasn't that
terrible? Over the edge in Rubidge Kloof with a baby inside her.
And while all this is going on there is Miss Deborah in her wheelchair. And then the biggest question of all: Why had he told him,
Booitjie, about all those terrible things that happened there on
Verlorevlei? It wasn't his business. What must he do with all that?

The only thing Booitjie could think of was that he would pray
for the Oubaas next Sunday when he sat in church because he
could see that the old man was very sorry about all that he did. Ja!
That had been something all right: seeing a White man cry like
that, like a baby. And him holding him like he was one! Ja – that
was maybe the strangest thing of all. If only the old man could
cry like that on Judgment Day then maybe God would also feel

sorry and forgive him because when a person was really sorry you must forgive them. He strengthened his resolve to pray very hard for Gerhardus Strydom in church.

As it turned out Booitjie had every reason to remember that resolution because when he returned to the house the following late afternoon to take over from the two women he found two cars parked outside, the women from the location crying in the kitchen and Mrs Kloppers and the doctor talking with hushed voices in the dining room. Gerhardus Strydom was dead. He had suffered another stroke in the afternoon. Booitjie never went back into the bedroom. When Mrs Kloppers found him in the kitchen she asked one of the women to fetch her handbag from the lounge while she told Booitjie about the old man's death and thanked him for all he had done for her father. Although it was only the middle of the month she paid him off with a full month's pay plus a bonus of an extra month's wages.

The funeral was held a few days later. Together with the two women from the location and a lorry-load of farm workers from Verlorevlei – all of them standing at a respectful distance behind the mourners at the graveside – Booitjie watched the Oubaas's coffin being lowered into the ground. Deborah Strydom and her sister Hannah were lying there waiting for him. Would they all see each other there on the other side? And if they did, what then? No, wragty, he really felt sorry for the Oubaas. Studying the White mourners carefully Booitjie realised that he had seen pictures of many of them during those sessions with the photo albums – quite a few of them when they were still only little children. Ja! What would they say if they knew what he knew? Because he could tell stories about quite a few of them as well! If there was one thing that Booitjie had learnt during those sessions with the photo albums it was that White people in their big houses got up to as much mischief as went on in the matchbox houses of the location. But they needn't worry. Their stories were safe with him. In the years that followed there were many times when he had been tempted to impress others with what he knew, but he had always stopped himself in time. He was sure that was what the Oubaas would have wanted.

And now, fifty years later, here he was again in that same room where he had sat with the Oubaas on the last night of his life. On that occasion, sitting on his own bed when the old man had finished his story and gone to sleep, Booitjie had watched the first light of day seep into the room. This time he was sitting on an upturned old paint tin watching the last light of day fade slowly. He knew he should get up and head home but stayed on just a little longer. Yes, he had prayed hard for Baas Gerrie on that next Sunday. Had it made any difference? Had God heard him? He hoped so, because in spite of everything Baas Gerrie had been a good man.

It was the complaining voices of a group of woman passing outside – they were obviously just back from the veld and were headed home with heavy loads of firewood on their heads – that got him struggling to his feet. For a few seconds he thought he would have to sit down again because his legs felt so weak, but after steadying himself he crossed the creaking floorboards to the door, then turned left down the long corridor to the back door. And after that very carefully – because the hand railing that used to be there was gone – he went down the steps to the yard and through the gate, which he closed behind him, and continued on down the road. He never once looked back. He had tried to remember the Oubaas's story and that was the most he could do. Waiting for him there on the road was the same thought that had kept him company on his way to the house:

. . . like mist, like the morning mist, all that pain, and joy and sorrow . . . gone

Shuffling along he spoke his last thought aloud:

'You have lived a long time Booitjie Barends and now, at the end of it, you still understand nothing.'

PART II

FACT AND FICTION

'Fact and Fiction' is composed of two documents that follow this note in sequence.

I have been keeping notebooks for virtually all of my writing life and the entries that make up 'Pages from a Notebook' come from one of them. A year after making those entries in my then current notebook I developed one element of the story therein – the facts – into the fictional narrative that follows: 'To whom it MUST concern'.

PAGES FROM A NOTEBOOK

11th June

I woke up this morning on the coast of southern California to an
overcast grey day and my seventieth birthday. I feel good about it.
It comes after a lunatic year in which I directed five productions
of my play *Sorrows and Rejoicings* on three continents – an exercise
that lived up to the title of the play in every sense of the word. It
left me physically and emotionally drained and made it very easy
for me at the end of it to decide that my days as a director were
over in much the same way that I decided a few years ago that I
would not do any more acting. I have no doubts about those
decisions. I've never had much of an opinion of myself in either
of those two roles. They had been forced on me in my early years
of making theatre in South Africa when I discovered that no one
wanted to touch the plays that I wanted to write. I had no choice
really but to get up there and have a go at it myself. What surprises
me is that I stayed up there for so long because I don't think I have
the right temperament for either acting or directing.

There are a few other resolutions as well, and taken together
they have given me a sense of adventure as I face up to whatever
time is left to me but now without any clutter to my essential
identity as a writer. I've reinforced that sense of adventure by
replacing the rickety old table I've been working on up to now
with a beautiful, solid slab of mahogany on four legs – my new
'home', the safest place in my universe because when I sit here I
know with something approaching conviction who and what I am.
That year of rehearsal rooms and nerve-wrecking and depressing

openings – I never learnt how to cope with them! – gave me no chance
to write. All I could do in the succession of hotel rooms I lived in
were a few vacuous entries in this notebook and a lot of yearning
for the time when I would be free once again to explore that ultimate
terra incognito, that most outer of all outer spaces – the blank page.

So here it is, the moment I anticipated so longingly during that
muscle-cramping year and the question of course is: What now?
It's not an intimidating question. I don't think there has ever been
a time when I didn't have at least half a dozen stories that I knew I
had to tell sooner or later. I could page back through this notebook
and find many entries shortlisting the 'appointments I have to keep'.
The trouble is that without exception it has never been left to me
to decide when that should be. Nothing would make me happier
than to make this the moment when I settle down to telling the story
of a hot summer's afternoon I spent with my dead and dear friend
Barney Simon in the garden of The Ashram – my Port Elizabeth
home – watching birds and talking about our lives and work. It would
be a celebration of one of the abiding passions of my life – bird-
watching – and of one of my most important friendships. But this
is not its moment because it's the story of Pumla Lolwana that is
commanding my attention this morning. It is just over a year and a
half since I read about her and her three children for the first time.
When I did I immediately recognised it as one of those stories I
would have an appointment with some day. This is what I read:

December 12, 2000

Mother, 3 children die in track suicide

Cape Town | Tuesday

*A MOTHER with a child on her back and two toddlers in her arms
stood on the tracks in front of an oncoming train – and when the five-
year-old child tried to scurry away, she pulled him back before the*

family was pulverised under the train's wheels, Die Burger *newspaper reported.*

The seriously traumatised train driver looked on helplessly as Pumla Lolwana (35), from the Samora Machel squatter camp, and her three children, Lindani (2), Andile (3) and Sesanda (5), died on the railway line between Philippi and Nyanga on the Cape Flats on Friday afternoon.

By Monday night nobody had claimed the bodies of the mother and her three children from the Salt River mortuary. The reason for her suicide, barely two weeks before Christmas, still remains a mystery.

Metro Rail confirmed to Die Burger *that Lolwana apparently committed suicide. "The train driver is receiving counselling. He is extremely traumatised, because he saw the drama play out in front of him and wasn't able to stop the train in time," Metro Rail representative Daphne Kayster said.*

An industrial social worker who works with train drivers told Die Burger *that many people use suicide in front of oncoming suburban trains as their 'way out' when personal problems get too much.*

Statistics published at the beginning of this month indicate that approximately 400 people die on the train tracks between Cape Town and Khayelitsha every year.

According to an eyewitness, one of the children managed to escape from his mother's arms. However, she pulled him back and held tightly on to him while the train sped closer. She made no attempt to get away or save her children.

Jaqueline van Rensburg, industrial social worker, who treats up to 15 train drivers a month after accidents, told Die Burger *that the drivers work under extremely difficult circumstances and feel guilty whenever anybody dies under their train.*

"The drivers feel very guilty because they have absolutely no control over the train. A train needs up to 300m to come to a stop. They can't swerve. They very much want to prevent the accident, but they are powerless.

"Some of the train drivers whom I have spoken to say they always

wonder about the victims' families and put themselves in that person's
shoes. In the long term these incidents have a negative impact on train
drivers."

The original is a file in my computer – I read the story in the
internet edition of the *Mail & Guardian*. I have now copied it out,
word for word, by hand, into this notebook. I did that because I
feel the need to possess it at a very personal level, to make it a part
of my life. Having done that I ask myself, yet again: This moment
of 'recognition' that has been such a recurring experience in my
writing life . . . what is it all about? How does it work? Why is it
that certain stories, faces or incidents in the thousands that crowd
my daily life will separate themselves from the others and take on
an imperative quality that demands that I deal with them and in
my case that obviously means writing about them. In 1988, at a
time when reports of the latest horrors of Apartheid were
crowding out each other on the front pages of our local Port
Elizabeth newspaper, it was a little three-inch item hidden away on
the back pages that really stopped me and made me read it again
and then again. The headline story on the front page was about
the massacre of twenty people when the police opened fire on a
funeral procession of a political activist. I of course read it and
was horrified but I moved on until I came to the story of Anela
Myalatya, a school teacher in a small country town who had been
necklaced by an angry mob because the word had gone around
that he was an informer. After reading it several times I fetched a
pair of scissors, cut it out and pasted it into my notebook.

Is it as simple as Stalin's cynical remark that a thousand deaths
are a statistic and one death a tragedy? That of course is what a
writer is always looking for – a strong story with an unhappy
ending. In my case however I know that there is also something
else at work, something less easy to define. It involves one of my
more important instincts as a writer because it has chosen the
stories I decided to tell. What I recognised in that image, face,

incident or three-inch newspaper story that stopped me is that it held out the possibility of looking at something in myself even though in most cases I was not aware of this at the time. Only afterwards did I realise that they were a shield I had held up so that I could slay a private Medusa. That was certainly the case with Anela Myalatya. *'My Children! My Africa!'*, the play I went on to write based on that three-inch item in the newspaper is a very political statement about a moment in my country's history, but also an intensely personal one. I have correctly described Mr M — the school teacher in my play — as an attempt at self-portraiture. His passions for learning and language, his belief in evolution rather than violent revolution … all of those faiths and qualities, as well as his serious flaws, are mine. I was not consciously aware of any of this when I started writing the play. In fact, if I had had the deliberate intention of doing that I doubt very much if that play or any of the others would have been written. Those 'intentions' are secrets that must be kept from even the writer himself.

So this morning it is Pumla Lolwana's story that I will try to live with. Somewhere in his writing Rilke advises a young poet to strive for a degree of innocence when he confronts blank paper and the start of a new adventure. I am not young and innocence is hard to come by now — so many words on paper lie behind this moment! — but I know it is good advice and I will try as hard as I can to follow it. In this instance I am certainly innocent of intentions or expectations. I don't know what will come, if anything, out of that newspaper story.

13th June

My usual sunset walk along the beach in the late afternoon and for a change the sky was clear; at this time of the year the sun usually sets behind a bank of fog waiting far out on the horizon to come drifting in during the night. After a few days of strong

spring tides and heavy surf the sea was again very calm with hardly
enough energy in it to uncurl a few small waves close inshore. In
the two years that I've been here I've never seen a really wild sea
like the ones I grew up with in the Eastern Cape of South Africa
when south-Atlantic gales lashed the coast. Half way along my
walk I did something that doesn't come easily to me in America:
I switched off my neurotic obsession with time which in this
instance meant regulating my walk so that I would be back in time
for one of the major items in my daily schedule – the BBC World
News broadcast at 6pm. Instead I sat down on the sand with no
other intention than to watch the setting sun. The last time I did
that was in the Karoo, in Nieu Bethesda, on my walks in the
koppies around the village when I would choose a convenient sun-
warmed rock and sit down and let time pass, just 'be' to the extent
that my restless nature is capable of that meditative state. Here on
the beach, as so many times in the Karoo, it was a gentle breeze,
this one off the sea, playing on my skin that turned the mystery
of time and its passing into a physical experience. The sunset was
simple and serene – a huge smoky orange globe trailing a wake of
golden light on the sea as it dropped slowly to the horizon.
I started thinking about Pumla Lolwana again.

The morning session at my table had started off with a another
close reading of the newspaper story. I took up each sentence and
looked at it as carefully as I do the beautiful wave-polished pebbles
I pick up on my beach walks and, just as I do then, I held on to each
sentence for a few seconds, turning it over and over so as to examine
it still more carefully before putting it back in its place on the page
and moving on. The one sentence I couldn't let go of easily, that I kept
going back to and looking at again and again was the opening one.

*A MOTHER with a child on her back and two toddlers in her arms
stood on the tracks in front of an oncoming train — and when the five-
year-old child tried to scurry away, she pulled him back before the
family was pulverised under the train's wheels.*

My mind stumbled and fell over itself in trying to deal with
that sentence. No matter how hard I tried I couldn't take it in,
truly understand it in a way that made it possible for me to move
on. Was it because I couldn't 'see' it? The sentence is profoundly
disturbing, it has a fierce energy in it, but when I tried to turn it
into a picture, my mind refused to move, all it could do was stare
at the horror of it. Because the idea alone — a mother commits
suicide and kills her three children with herself — is not enough
for me as a writer. Ideas never have been. Some sort of picture or
image has been the starting point to everything I have written and
I need one now if I am going to do something with that newspaper report, but try as I may I can't break the paralysing effect of
that sentence. Pumla Lolwana is shrouded in a darkness my
imagination can't penetrate. I've tried to unblock it by imagining
the sound of those few dreadful seconds — the children's cries,
specially the little boy struggling to get away because he knew
what was his mother was trying to do, and their names, their
beautiful names! Surely she called them out when she tried to
comfort and calm them as the train got closer, and then the noise
of the train itself, the hooter, the screech of brakes — but even that
ploy didn't work.

I went through the story again hoping I might have overlooked
something that would set me off, but it was a pointless exercise;
I already knew the story by heart and I knew there wasn't anything
that would help me start to build a picture of her. With a growing
sense of frustration I put her aside and turned to other work.

Sitting there on the beach at the end of the day, watching the
sky fade through a spectrum of soft pastel colours, I had to ask
myself why my imagination wasn't working for me this time. Why
wasn't it taking control of the facts as laid out in the newspaper
story and creating a plausible fiction as it had done so many times
in the past fifty years of writing. I'd never known it to hesitate in
that way before. Why now? Was it that it felt it didn't have the
right — that much vaunted writer's liberty and licence — to do that

this time? Why not just go back to my table tonight and, in exactly the same way as I put the school teacher of that three-inch newspaper story into a tired old double-breasted suit in my imagination, see that young mother standing there on the tracks waiting barefoot for the train? That one little detail might be the trigger I was looking for.

That little surge of hope didn't last long. I had a growing sense that in fact this time I was without any rights to liberty or licence. Apart from the fact that suicide is something I know I will never understand, will always be a mystery to me, there is something about the story of Pumla Lolwana and her three children that would make feeding it to my writer's ego very obscene.

As for just witnessing it ... I can't even do that because I don't in fact know if she was wearing shoes or if she and the children were barefoot.

14th June

As an alternative to the beach I sometimes walk next to the railway line that connects San Diego to Los Angeles. The regular traffic on this line is the blue and white Coaster, a local suburban commuter train with a blaring organ-like note for a hooter, and less frequently the blue and silver Surfliner which goes with only a few stops all the way to Los Angeles. A few times during the day and night, long freight trains also travel along this line. I saw a real beauty yesterday — forty-five coaches and wagons, all with the name 'Barnum and Bailey Circus' proudly emblazoned on their sides. The walk is a lovely but mildly illegal one. There are signs all along the way in Spanish and English warning that there is danger and that I am trespassing on railway property, but none of the joggers and walkers who use the path pay any attention to them. Along this stretch of the line the tracks are only a few yards in from the edge of a cliff — there is just enough room for the footpath and a swathe of purple Statice that are in bloom at the moment and clumps of elegant Pampas grass. Standing at the edge of the cliff, you have the delight of gulls and pelicans floating by at chest level. A few hundred feet below, a mostly blue and smiling Pacific Ocean rolls onto a clean white beach, its only debris those beautiful stones I pick up and discard and clumps of kelp. Dolphins play in these waters and at the right time of the year whales can be spotted on their way to and from their mating grounds off the coast of Mexico. There is one other very southern Californian detail in this scene: the little black figures on their long boards, waiting for the perfect wave along the line where the surf first heaves up to come rolling in.

The passengers on the trains headed north to Oceanside, San Clemente, San Juan Capistrano, Irvine, Santa Ana, Anaheim, Fullerton and Los Angeles – all of them neat Spanish-style stations with attractive floral features – enjoy wonderful views of the sea and coastline. It is a very different experience to that of the commuters travelling from Khayelitsha, through Nonkqubela, Nolungile, Mandalay, Philippi, Nyanga, Heideveld, Netreg, Bonteheuwel, Langa, Mutual, Ysterplaat, Paarden Eiland, to Cape Town. A friend in Cape Town sent me a copy of a video which is shown to train drivers on this route as part of their six-month training programme. It takes you from the driver's point of view, from Khayelitsha all the way in to Cape Town – a fifty-minute ride through a landscape of soul-crushing squalor. At the best of times the sandy, wind-blown Cape Flats through which the route runs has little or no appeal; the ulcerous squatter camps of miserable shanties and pondoks that now line this route into the mother city are dumping grounds of hopeless human lives. Our proud slogan 'The Cape of Good Hope' is a cruel misnomer for the world these people live in.

Thirty years ago, in my play *Boesman and Lena* I made a drunk and embittered Boesman describe their pondok on the mudflats of the Swartkops River as 'White man's rubbish.' In a paroxysm of self-hatred he goes on to say: 'we pick it up, we wear it, we eat it, we're made of it now ... we're White man's rubbish'. That was the old Apartheid South Africa. This is the brave new South Africa. The people who live in those pondoks on the Cape Flats – structures every bit as flimsy and useless against the elements as the one Boesman built – can't single out the White man as the source of their rubbish anymore, but in essence the refrain is the same: they live in a world made out of rubbish, they are the rubbish of that world.

Boesman and Lena was my first deep journey into the world of the pondok, a world that had fascinated me from my childhood when I used to accompany my Mom to a butcher in a humble little Coloured settlement on the outskirts of Port Elizabeth to buy black-market meat for our boarding house during the strictly rationed years of the Second World War. The nearest I can get to explaining that fascination – it is there even in southern California when I see the simple homes of Mexican labourers – is to point to the elemental power and simplicity that the gestures and things in those lives acquire because they are so poverty stricken, so reduced to essentials. All my life, and I don't really know why, it has been those humble and desperate little worlds that have fired my imagination; I have studied them and tried to imagine my way into their secret life as eagerly and passionately as others do with the palaces and mansions of the mighty.

What fascinates me as a writer is the way in which the destitution of those lives can sometimes invest simple things and events, even simple gestures, with huge transcendent values and resonances. When Lena breaks and shares her crust of brown bread with Outa, as they sit huddled together in the cold of the Swartkops mudflats, it is the profound simplicity of those elements that turn that moment into a mass, a bitter celebration of her life. That crust of brown bread and mug of bitter and black tea become sacramental: 'Bitter and black,' she says. 'The bread should have bruises ... it's my life Outa.' A loaf of fresh white bread in the hands of a comfortable suburban housewife could never resonate in that way.

In writing that play I put together all the clues I had accumulated over the years in trying to find my way into the heart of that reality. I believe I succeeded. I revisited that play recently with a student production at the University of California in San Diego and I can say now with conviction that there are no falsehoods in it. So having made that imaginative journey on the mudflats, shouldn't it now be possible for me, in a similar fashion, to crawl into the pondok in the Samora Machel informal settlement that Pumla Lolwana and her three children lived in? The story of South African poverty, like the story of poverty anywhere, is made up of a few very stark elements, starting with hunger and ending, as must have been the case with Pumla Lolwana, with a loss of hope. Within that terrible little span of human experience there are a few variables that can be assembled in different patterns. In her case those variables most likely included the loss of the breadwinner, her man, the father of her children. It could have been a death — those 'informal settlements' are violent worlds — it could have been desertion, a man looking for his 'way out' when the burden of a wife and three children became too much. Given those possibilities can't I now just get on with it for God's sake and give Pumla Lolwana a fictional reality and deal with her in the way that I did with Boesman and Lena? I wish I could, but the answer is again 'no'. Boesman and Lena wanted to live. As devastating as that night on the mudflats had been for both of them, they are on their feet at the end, they walk away from that cold campfire and the dead Black man even though it is a walk into darkness. Implicit in that walk is their will to live, an unconscious act of faith in the next day's sunrise. That is the fundamental act of faith in my life: there will be a tomorrow worth living. That is why I shied away from an earlier challenge to confront final despair. The real Helen Martins of my play *The Road To Mecca* died in agony, caustic soda eating away her insides, because she had lost faith in herself. That is not how my telling of her extraordinary story ends. I used my 'liberty and licence' as a storyteller to create a note of affirmation after she confronts the extinction of her creativity. I can't play any fictional games with Pumla Lolwana. That moment when she stands on the railway lines, fiercely holding on to her children, is too final.

17th June

I was back next to the tracks again this afternoon. I took a moment during my walk when I was sure there were no trains coming to stand between them and stare along their length. I had never given them a second thought before reading Pumla Lolwana's story; now, those two parallel rails of steel fascinate me. There is something hypnotic and strangely menacing in the illusion of convergence as they stretched away from me. The same thing has happened to the trains that come charging past on my walks. They are huge double-decker leviathans with the driver's cab up at the top level. Up until now I've enjoyed them innocently as images of energy and splendour which is how the old steam engines of my youth used to thrill me when I was growing up in Port Elizabeth. Now they also have become very unnerving, their power and momentum, their unstoppable force, very frightening. The adrenaline rush that comes as they thunder past is no longer the elating thrill of my boyhood, it is fear.

One of them, a northbound Coaster, passed me on this afternoon's walk. I heard it before I saw it — a raucous blare from its horn as it left the Penasquitos marsh and came rushing out from under the road bridge. Although I couldn't see the driver up in his cab I gave him a wave as the train passed. I don't suppose he even noticed me.

The Cape Town commuter trains are single-deckers, so those drivers do not ride as high and mighty as their American cousins.

By comparison with them the driver of the train that killed Pumla Lolwana and her children would have had a very intimate relationship with her as she stood there waiting for him. His was most probably the last human face she saw, provided of course that she kept her eyes open until the end. It is a thought that stops time: the two of them looking at each other, seeing each other, locked into a moment that will end the life of the mother and her children and scar his forever. The rest of my walk is a blank. The thought of those few seconds between the woman and the train driver haunted me all the way back to this table. I went back to the newspaper report and read:

> *The train driver is receiving counselling. He is extremely traumatised, because he saw the drama play out in front of him and wasn't able to stop the train in time.*

It takes three hundred meters for one of these trains travelling at a speed of seventy kph to stop. But he most probably didn't. The instructions to the driver in the event of an accident on this line are very specific:

If the driver is between stations he must not stop. The body will be behind him and he must continue to the next station. There he must report the incident via radio, and have the police and rescue services called.

I've never really given the driver much thought, but now it occurs to me that he could possibly help me see her. If I could live through a night on the Swartkops mudflats with Boesman and Lena then couldn't I sit in the cab with the train driver for that fatal afternoon run from Khayelitsha to Cape Town? Unlike the mother, so emphatically identified by her name, 'Pumla Lolwana', and her children, his very anonymity is a help. It is in fact hugely liberating. For the first time since starting to live with that newspaper story I feel a surge of energy and excitement because I realise I am free to create a fictional identity.

So here goes: His name will be 'Roelf Visagie', a strong, no-nonsense, down-to-earth Afrikaans name. The railways in South Africa have always been the preserve of the Afrikaner and if there is one South African identity I empathise with it is them – my mother's people. I know I've chosen a good name because without any effort on my side 'Roelf Visagie' has attracted to itself images from the life of a friend of mine in Port Elizabeth, a fishing companion of many years. The training video that was sent me from Cape Town included interviews with and images of the drivers at the controls of the train. Their faces were those of decent but deeply troubled men who had not been able to stop the train in time; they had all had their 'hits' – the word used by one of them to describe those accidents. They spoke in muted tones about what it meant because '... it's a life you're taking, another human being ... and you never forget the first one – no matter how many hits you have after that, you never forget the first one. Doesn't matter what it is – a cow, or a dog or an old man – it's all the same, it's a life you've taken.' My Roelf Visagie would be at home in their company, drinking a cold Castle or a brandy and Coke and talking about the general fuck-up of the world. For all his rough edges, my fishing friend in Port Elizabeth was also a good man; he had the same reverence for life that I saw in the faces and heard in the voices of the men in the training video.

So I decided it was going to be my Roelf Visagie's first hit – that is the dangerous side of writing, playing God with the fictional lives you've created.

He of course had no idea of what I had in store for him that Friday afternoon. If anything his life felt and looked particularly good as he settled down in the driver's cab for the run to Cape Town. He had a devoted wife and two lovely children – a boy and a girl – a nice house in a quiet suburb and to complete the picture he was a White man with a job and a reasonably well-paid one at that with a pension fund and medical scheme – no mean achievement in the new South Africa. But what really gave his spirits a lift when he got the signal to pull out of Khayelitsha station that Friday afternoon were his fishing prospects for the coming weekend. He was going to join two fishing buddies for a trip up the West Coast to look for Steenbras. They were going to make a whole weekend of it, sleeping on the beach and returning for work early on Monday. When the train pulled into Nonkqubela station Roelfie was imagining the campfire, the lovely barbecue smell of chops and boerewors sizzling away on the coals. At Nolungile it was that electrifying moment when a fishing-reel ratchet suddenly starts screaming in the middle of the night and, still half asleep, you scramble for your rod because you know a Steenbras has picked you up. The next stations were Mandalay and Philippi and once again the train pulled in and pulled out on time and Roelf Visagie, with his hands on the brake and accelerator, luxuriated in the sense that his life, like his train, was under control.

The training video gives a good picture of what the drivers on this Khayelitsha–Cape Town route have to contend with. There are of course fences on each side of the track that are meant obviously to keep people off it, but these have been broken down or torn through in places so as to provide a shortcut from the squatter camp on one side to the one on the other side. In the video one constantly sees people walking next to the tracks or making suicidal dashes across them in front of the oncoming train. With all that going on Roelf Visagie would hardly have noticed the woman way ahead of him waiting quietly on the side. But even if he had seen her standing there – a mother with a baby on her back and two children in her arms – what of it? He must have seen at least half a dozen like her already on this run. In any case – come now man! – a mother and her children? She's not going to go and do something stupid – until suddenly there she is in front of him with one of the children struggling to break loose, looking up at him, and Roelf Visagie starts to live through a few seconds that will haunt him for the rest of his life. He has his hand on the brake, his foot on the hooter, he is shouting and swearing, but it makes no difference. His life is out of control. It is over in a flash.

It wouldn't have been long before a crowd would have gathered there, pressed against the fence, or crawling through the holes in it for a closer look at the remains of Pumla Lolwana and her three children. And angry! Oh yes, very angry. Very loud angry voices. 'Haai Liewe Here. Look at them! How many is it? A mother and three children for God's sake. Is there no bloody justice in the world? Didn't that bloody driver see her? Why didn't that fucking White man stop?'

That is why head office has ordered the drivers to just carry on to the next station in the event of an accident.

20th June

Another alternative to my beach walk is along a stretch of 'Historic Highway 101' as it skirts the Penasquitos Marsh. This one gives me a chance to study the wonderful variety of water birds in the marsh. It is also a very schizoid experience as it involves walking the line between two starkly contrasting worlds: stretching away from me on one side is the serene marsh, its self-contained silence broken only by the high, piping calls of curlews and sandpipers, and on the other side, just a few feet away from me as I walk along the very narrow verge, the never ending rush and roar of traffic on the Highway. On this evening's walk the birds were all there in the distance waiting in the muddy channels of the marsh for the incoming tide to reach them: herons and egrets, Long-billed Curlews and whimbrels and godwits, sandpipers and plovers. I had my binoculars focused on a Great Blue Heron when a blue and white Coaster rode into its field of vision. Distance and the soft light of the evening had once again made it very innocent, a thing of beauty; it could so easily have been a little toy train on the floor of a young boy's bedroom and not the terrible instrument a despairing soul would use to end a life.

Back at my table later I read:

> The train driver is receiving counselling. He is extremely traumatised, because he saw the drama play out in front of him and wasn't able to stop the train in time.

... and then at the end of the story:

> Jaqueline van Rensburg, industrial social worker, who treats up to 15 train drivers a month after accidents, told Die Burger that the drivers work under extremely difficult circumstances and feel guilty whenever anybody dies under their train.

In the training video the drivers talk about the trauma. The advice given to them by the social worker is to talk about it, the sooner the better, and to anyone who will listen.

That is the advice a sympathetic Miss Jacqueline van Rensburg gives a hesitant Mr Visagie when he sits down awkwardly in her office for a counselling session. The likes of Roelfie Visagie do not take easily to counselling and even more so when it comes from a woman, but Miss van Rensburg knows this – he is not the first driver to come to her for help.

'Whatever you are feeling don't keep it bottled up inside you Mr Visagie. Talking will help you take control of the experience and put it behind you so that you can get on with your life.'

But Mr Visagie does not find it easy. It takes a lot of patience on her side and gentle nudging, before the words start to come, very haltingly at first as he clumsily feels his way into the emotional chaos inside him. She listens and watches carefully as he talks, reading signs of anger and confusion, pain and guilt.

'Ja, I know Miss. I know it's not really my fault, everybody keeps telling me that, you, my wife, the other drivers – some of them have already had as many as twenty hits! – ja, that's that they call it, a hit. "It's because it's your first one Visagie," they say to me, "that's why it's so hard. But give it time. You'll get over it." I get so the hell in when people tell me that Miss. Ja. You as well. I know you are all just trying to help me so I don't mean to be offensive but I mean what the hell, if it's not my fault – and I don't need anybody to tell me that anymore! – then whose fault is it? Ja, why doesn't somebody try telling me that for a change instead of all this …'

(He leaves the sentence unfinished. Miss van Rensburg interprets the restless movement of his hands as the need for a cigarette. She tells him he can smoke if he wants to. He shakes his head.)

'Must we point our fingers at Metrorail? Ja, why not? They don't fix up the fences on the side of the tracks where the people have broken them down? God didn't just put her down there on those tracks you know. She and her children crawled through one of those holes to get there. I've given up reporting them anymore because nobody listens. Or maybe it's the Government to blame. Maybe they should take some time off from driving around in their big Mercedes Benzes and give those people decent houses to live in. You take off some time one day Miss and go and look at those pondoks. My dog's kennel in our backyard is better than what those people is living in. And then of course there's the woman herself. Because don't think I've forgotten her. I wish I could. But even if I could my wife wouldn't let me because that's who she points the finger at. Ja, good old Lynette.

"She's the one who did it Roelfie darling. Nobody dragged her and her children onto the railway lines. I don't know how a mother could do a thing like that but she did. I bet you anything you like she was drunk. So you see liefling, it's not your fault."

'Just like that. I got it from her again this morning. I had another bad night you see. I took the pills the doctor gave me, but the trouble is sort of … ag what the hell … I'm sort of frightened of going to sleep because even with the pills if I wake up it

starts again, over and over – I'm looking at the tracks and then ...
I swear to God I didn't see her until suddenly there she is in front
of me, waiting for me, with the children. Anyway, that is how my
day started – with Lynette walking around the room, getting ready
to go to her job at Pick 'n Pay and I can see she's the hell in
because she also didn't get much sleep because of me but she is
trying so hard to hide it while she tells Roelfie darling that it isn't
his fault and how could a mother do a thing like that and please
liefling go and see you doctor again and ask him for bigger pills
because these little ones isn't knocking you out ... And while I'm
sitting there on the bed watching her and listening I'm also seeing
pictures of that world on the side of the tracks and it makes me
naar, you know, like I want to vomit because it's all there inside me
now, ja, that my Christmas bonus this year I got a whole rotten
stinking bloody squatter camp inside me, choking me so badly I
can't tell Lynette to shut the fuck up because she doesn't know
what she is talking about, she doesn't know anything. But even if
she did, even if she did turn off the hair dryer and give me a
chance for a change, what would I say to her? What can I say to
you Miss who finds it so easy to tell me it wasn't my fault because
she was "looking for a way out of her troubles"? Do you know
about those "personal problems"? If I ever get back to driving you
must take a ride with me one day – Khayelitsha to Cape Town. I'll
point out the beauty spots. We'll do it in winter when a good
Cape storm has left that whole world under six inches of water.
Then you will see them, in the early morning, the mothers with
their babies in their arms standing outside their pondoks because
there was no place to lie down inside. That's when you start to ask
questions Miss. How long have they been standing? All night?
How they going to cook food for the children?'

[Pause. This time he lights a cigarette. Miss van Rensburg
revises a mental note she was going to put into his file: it's not
anger she's watching, it's rage.

'So you see Miss, why she did it is not the problem. Ag no, who want to live like that? Who want tomorrow if it means your children are going to be living like that? And while they're living like that, getting murdered, or raped or ending up with AIDS and everything else. No, to hell with it. I understand why she did it. Any sensible mother would drag her kids through a hole in the fence onto those tracks if that is all they could hope for. No Miss, my problem is why the hell did she have to go and choose my train? Why didn't she wait for the guy with his twenty hits? He knows how to forget her. Instead she chooses me. No, don't shake your head! She was standing there waiting for me and I couldn't say "No thank you lady, not today". That's what people like you don't understand. There was no way out for me Miss. I couldn't swerve, I couldn't stop the fucking train. Ja, there's another joke for you if you want one. "The Controls!" "The train driver must remain in control of the train at all times." Bull shit! I had no more control over the train when she stood there than I did over the day I was born. If you really want to know something Miss, I'm not so sure anymore I got control over anything. And let me tell you something else: I'm not the only one. Ja. You too! Sitting there behind your desk and looking like you're "in control"! That driver's cab is a trap Miss, and we're all in there one way or another. We can see it coming, we're heading towards it at ninety kilometres an hour, but we can't swerve and the instructions from head office is: "Don't stop, just leave the bloody mess behind you and carry on."'

And that is as far as I go with Roelf Visagie. I could follow him out of that counselling session into the rest of his life, the passing of time that will turn his raw wound into a scar, sit one night around a campfire with Des and Dennis waiting for a ratchet to scream — but in doing that I would also be leaving behind the mess on the tracks between Philippi and Nyanga and I can't do that.

24th June

For a change I was in a train, a Surfliner headed north to Los
Angeles. I was on my way to watch an understudy rehearsal and to
say goodbye to the wonderful cast of my play *Sorrows and Rejoicings*
which was in the last week of its run in LA. I settled back in my
comfortable business-class seat determined for once to do nothing
other than look out of the window and enjoy the long stretch of
beautiful scenery on this route. Old habits don't break easily
though, so I did have my notebook and my pen in my lap just in
case. And just as well. Darwin called it his 'cacoethes scribendi' his
incurable itch to write. I suffer from the same complaint. It wasn't
long before I had forgotten about the scenery and was scribbling
away.

It had started with a delay at Oceanside station because of
work on the track. It made me wonder if there had been a parallel
experience for the passengers in the coaches behind Roelf Visagie?
Had they started looking out of the window as I had just done
wondering what had gone wrong and how long the delay would be
before the train started moving again? Then seeing officials
running around outside on the platform and hearing talk about a
woman and three children. It was a sobering and depressing
thought. It suggested that maybe that was all I could ever hope to
be – a passenger in the train that had killed a mother and her
children, getting scraps of second-hand news about their death
and impatient for the train to move on.

My return journey to San Diego was late at night and my
notebook was again in my lap because the itch to scratch away at a
blank page was even stronger than in the morning. The cab ride
from the station to the theatre had passed the County Courthouse
and that had immediately brought LaShanda Crozier back into my
life. Her story was carried by the LA Times ten days after I had
read about Pumla Lolwana. It was then just three days before
Christmas. Her story is also a file in my computer.

Friday, December 22, 2000

Troubled life led to 3 deaths

Tragedy: Many people saw LaShanda Crozier's personal and financial problems, but no sign that she would throw her two daughters off a courthouse ledge, then jump.

When LaShanda Crozier pushed her two daughters to their deaths off the downtown County Courthouse and followed them down, it ended a spell of economic and personal hardship, neighbors, relatives and authorities said Thursday. Crozier, 27, had talked of suffering a miscarriage that cost her a job, seeing her boyfriend lose a job, and facing eviction — the threat that brought her to the courthouse, they said.

Hours after reaching an out-of-court agreement with her landlord to gradually pay $925 in back rent, Crozier pushed daughters Breanna, 7, and Joan, 5, from the ninth-floor ledge and then jumped herself.

Her boyfriend, the girls' father, left the courthouse after the hearing and did not witness the deaths, authorities said. He said Thursday, "I have not come to terms with what happened to my children." He also said he was angry at Crozier, whom he described as selfish. "She should have called me at work."

Crozier owed back rent on the $400-a-month apartment unit near Exposition Park that she shared with the girls and their father.

In a hallway outside Courtroom 547 on Wednesday, as they waited for the judge, Crozier and landlord Raul Almendariz tried to negotiate an agreement. He offered to allow the family to stay in their cramped, ground-floor quarters if they would start paying weekly installments of about $150. As an alternative, Almendariz offered to let Crozier out of the lease — and the back payments — if she would move the family out right after Jan. 1.

Almendariz said Crozier wanted to stay, even though a recent rough patch had left the couple with little money.

He said the couple told him that Crozier had spent a few days in a hospital after losing a child to a miscarriage, and that the episode cost her a job cleaning rooms at a local hotel. The boyfriend said that he had lost one of his two jobs because of the Metropolitan Transportation Authority bus drivers strike and that his other job paid just $250 a week.

"She seemed embarrassed yesterday, about the whole situation," Almendariz said. "She didn't try to make any excuses at all. She said she would just like the opportunity to stay in the apartment and catch up on the rent."

Almendariz said he agreed. Crozier signed the court papers and headed outside and into the sunshine with her boyfriend and children in tow.

Stunned family members on Thursday described Crozier as a troubled woman who had struggled economically, emotionally and in a stormy relationship with her boyfriend. They said that in recent years she had occasionally given up custody of the two girls to an aunt, Marietta Snowden.

"She was sometimes unstable," said Snowden. "My niece was withdrawn."

Snowden also said she had been trying to retain custody of the two girls, citing her concerns about Crozier's relationship with her boyfriend, the poor living conditions at the apartment complex and Crozier's mental state. But "nobody listened, nobody listened, nobody listened," she said.

Snowden described Breanna as an outgoing tomboy who was fiercely protective of her little sister. Joan, she said, was shy and quiet, a "pretty little girl who loved to wear high-heeled sneakers".

Snowden said Breanna sensed there was something wrong with her mother and father. "She said, 'Auntie, I love my mama, but I don't want to stay with her.'"

Almendariz, like so many others who had crossed paths with Crozier, said that in recent days she had shown no signs of irrational behavior or flashes of anger or depression. There was nothing to signal that she was capable of pushing the two girls off a ledge and then jumping herself.

Witnesses later told police the two objects they saw Crozier push or throw over the ledge were the two girls.

Both landed on a fourth-floor ledge and were taken to County-USC Medical Center, where they died a short time later.

Crozier landed on the ground and was pronounced dead at the scene. Los Angeles police continued to investigate the matter Thursday, and court officials reviewed their files to glean hints to what might have prompted Crozier's actions.

Crozier was described by neighbors as friendly but quiet and somewhat guarded.

She and her boyfriend kept to themselves. And they argued occasionally behind closed doors, the neighbors said.

"They had their problems," said Zelaya, but no more than anyone else in the run-down building a block west of the Los Angeles Coliseum and the USC campus.

LAPD Capt. Charlie Beck said the boyfriend was trying in vain Thursday to come to terms with what had happened.

"He's doing awful," Beck said. "How do you even begin to understand the kind of pain that this is causing somebody?

"We will be talking to him again, see if he can put some shred of reason to this," said Beck. "But he didn't have anything he could offer . . . I don't think there is an answer for this that anyone but she will ever know."

Penelope Trickett, a developmental psychologist and professor of social work at USC, acknowledged the perplexing nature of cases in which suicidal parents choose to kill their children.

"I think it has something to do with a bond between parents and kids," she said. "The feeling you are one entity, you and your children, and that if there is no hope for you, there is no hope for the children."

Landlord Almendariz said he was haunted Thursday by his last image of Crozier.

As they left the courthouse, he had just given her older daughter Breanna a $20 bill and told her to share it with her little sister as a Christmas present. The little girl politely said "Thank you," and "Yes, I will," he said.

He said, Crozier seemed a little sad but nothing more.

"I wish I could have talked to her a little bit more. Told her, you know, things are going to be OK, that people have their ups and downs. I wish there was something somebody could have done to help," he added.

"Somebody should have known how depressed she was."

Apart from its own unique horror, what struck me about this story as compared with that of Pumla Lolwana was the wealth of personal detail and the expressions of concern and sorrow by neighbours, relatives and authorities. What a vivid hint there is for example of the characters and relationship of Breanna and Joan and in contrast the absence of any detail about Andile, Lindani and Sesanda. I did a word count: 1266 for LaShanda Crozier, 408 for Pumla Lolwana.

I have also tried to establish if there had been any follow-up stories about Pumla Lolwana that might possibly have given some information about her life and circumstances, but I couldn't find any. I have to ask myself: Is there any significance in this? Do we South Africans put a lower value on life? Have we been so insensitised, so numbed by our long history of violence, the prevalence of poverty and famine in Africa, the constant bombardment by the media of stories and images of starving mothers and children on this God-forsaken continent that the death of another mother and her three children merits only a bland and relatively impersonal report which gives more space to the trauma of the train driver than to the victims of the tragedy? I almost regret now that I know their names. It fostered the illusion that I could somehow get to know them, understand something about what happened on that Friday afternoon. Anonymity would have disillusioned me of that and made even more starkly clear the destitution of that tragic family.

At the end of *My Children! My Africa!*, just before he goes out to confront an angry mob in what amounts to an act of self-immolation, my Mr M bares his soul to the young Thami in a long monologue which ends with this passage:

'I was eight years old and we were on our way to a rugby match at Somerset East. The lorry stopped at the top of the mountain so that we could stretch our legs and relieve ourselves. It was a hard ride on the back of that lorry. The road hadn't been tarred yet. So there I was, eight years old and sighing with relief as I aimed for the

little bush. It was a hot day. The sun right over our heads ... not a cloud in the vast blue sky. I looked out ... it's very high up there at the top of the pass ... and there it was, stretching away from the foot of the mountain, the great pan of the Karoo ... stretching away forever it seemed into the purple haze and heat of the horizon. Something grabbed my heart at that moment, my soul, and squeezed it until there were tears in my eyes. I had never seen anything so big, so beautiful in all my life. I went to the teacher who was with us and asked him: "Teacher, where will I come to if I start walking that way?" ... and I pointed. He laughed. "Little man," he said, "that way is north. If you start walking that way and just keep on walking, and your legs don't give in, you will see all of Africa! Yes, Africa little man! You will see the great rivers of the continent: the Vaal, the Zambezi, the Limpopo, the Congo and then the mighty Nile. You will see the mountains: the Drakensberg, Kilimanjaro, Kenya and the Ruwenzori. And you will meet all our brothers: the little Pygmies of the forests, the proud Masai, the Watusi ... tallest of the tall and the Kikuyu standing on one leg like herons in a pond waiting for a frog." "Has teacher seen all that?" I asked. "No," he said. "Then how does teacher know it's there?" "Because it is all in the books and I have read the books and if you work hard in school little man, you can do the same without worrying about your legs giving in."

He was right Thami. I have seen it. It is all there in the books just as he said it was and I have made it mine. I can stand on the banks of all those great rivers, look up at the majesty of all those mountains, whenever I want to. It is a journey I have made many times. Whenever my spirit was low and I sat alone in my room, I said to myself: Walk Anela! Walk! ... and I imagined myself at the foot of the Wapadsberg setting off for that horizon that called me that day forty years ago. It always worked! When I left that little room, I walked back into the world a proud man, because I was an African and all the splendour was my birthright.

[Pause] I don't want to make that journey again Thami. There is someone waiting for me now at the end of it who has made a mockery of all my visions of splendor. He has in his arms my real birthright. I saw him on the television in the Reverend Mbopa's lounge. An Ethiopian tribesman, and he was carrying the body of a little child that had died of hunger in the famine ... a small bundle carelessly wrapped in a few rags. I couldn't tell how old the man was. The lines of despair and starvation on his face made him look as old as Africa itself.

He held that little bundle very lightly as he shuffled along to a mass grave, and

*when he reached it, he didn't have the strength to kneel and lay it down gently. . . .
He just opened his arms and let it fall. I was very upset when the programme
ended. Nobody had thought to tell us his name and whether he was the child's
father, or grandfather, or uncle. And the same for the baby! Didn't it have a name?
How dare you show me one of our children being thrown away and not tell me
its name! I demand to know who is in that bundle!*

*[Pause] Not knowing their names doesn't matter anymore. They are more than
just themselves. The tribesman and dead child do duty for all of us Thami. Every
African soul is either carrying that bundle or in it.*

*What is wrong with this world that it wants to waste you all like that . . .
my children . . . my Africa!"*

Standing there on the railway line between Philippi and
Nyanga, with her children in her arms, Pumla Lolwana joins that
Ethiopian tribesman with a matching and terrifying loneliness; a
Stabat Mater Dolarosa without a redeeming Christ on the cross.

27th June

It is either late at night or very early in the morning and I am lying
awake in bed. I resist looking at the luminous dial of my wrist
watch because I know that that will only make going back to sleep
more difficult. But for once I am not fretting about my insomnia, I
am listening to a freight train — it is heading south — I can both
hear and feel the vibrations of passing train traffic in my bedroom.
This is a long one and I try to count the individual trucks as they
trundle heavily over the bridge in the marsh, but after a few
seconds I lose count because whenever I hear a passing train these
days I always end up thinking about Pumla Lolwana. How close
was her pondok to the railway line? Did she lie awake at night
listening to passing trains? Is that how she got the idea? Playing
back the images I have of her final moments there is one which,
surprisingly and for reasons that elude me, I seem to have a dark

sympathy with, almost an understanding: it is the moment when Sesanda tried to escape and she pulled him back and held on to him fiercely as the train sped closer.

'If you live, so must I, but I can't, I can't ...'

And that last walk of hers with the children. It would have been dramatic to picture it in pouring rain, mother and children drenched to the skin, but that is not the case. That last walk was in bright and mild sunshine with just a gentle breeze blowing and hardly a cloud in the sky — I have the weather report for that day.

Women walking. Pumla Lolwana is not the only powerful and virtually nameless presence in my life. She has sisters. My note-books record a few other destitute women who have walked across my path leaving their shadows on my work. In August of 1965 I made this entry about a life I gave to an old African woman:

We picked her up about ten miles outside Cradock. She was carrying all her worldly possessions in a bundle on her head and an old shopping bag. I'd guess about seventy years old. Cleft palate. A very hot day.

Her story was that she had been chased off a farm after her husband's death about three days previously. She was walking to another farm where she had a friend. Later on she told us that she had nine children but didn't know where they were. She thought a few of them were in P.E.

After driving about fifteen miles it became obvious that she would never have reached her destination on foot that day. We asked her about this and she said she knew it and would have slept in one of the storm-water drains.

She cried frequently. The first time was when I took the bundle (it was very heavy) off her head and put it in the boot and she realised she was going to get a lift. She told May she couldn't believe it. 'It was like a dream.' Then in the car, telling her story, she cried again, May comforted her. Finally, when we reached the gate where she wanted to get off and I gave her two of the three shillings left in my pocket, she cried again. I put the bundle on her head; May carried the shopping bag down an embankment to the gate and set her on her way. My last image of her is the thin, scrawny ankles between her old shoes and the edge of her old skirt, trudging away into the bush.

I suppose she stopped to cry a little and then went on, cried again later and went on, went on and on.

Barney — about her bundle: 'She still has a use for the things in her life.' And just her life; still using it — feeding it, sleeping it, washing it.

Her bundle consisted of one of those heavy three-legged iron pots, a blanket and an old zinc bath full of other odds and ends — all this tired together with a dirty piece of flaxen twine. In the old shopping bag I spotted a bottle of tomato sauce and Barney spotted a packet of OMO.

Finally only this to say: that in that cruel walk under the blazing sun, walking from all of her life that she didn't have on her head, facing the prospect of a bitter Karoo night in a drain-pipe, in this walk there was no defeat — there was pain, and great suffering, but no defeat.

In 1968 this entry:

Another Coloured woman who might have been a model for my Lena. Lived somewhere in the bush along the Glendore Road. Worked for us for a short period about two years ago. Sense of appalling physical and spiritual destitution, of servility. Did the housework without a word or sound, without the slightest flicker of her 'self'. For some reason left us after about two months. Then some time later came back to see if we had any work. A stiflingly hot day ... Berg wind blowing. In the course of the few words I had with her she seemed to be in an even more desperate condition that when we had last seen her — not so much physically, though that was still there, but poverty is poverty and at its worst there are not grades — it was a sense of her disorientation, almost derangement, of only a fraction of herself committed to and involved in the world around her. After telling the woman we had no work, she left us to try a few other houses. An hour or so later, the heat even more fierce by then, I left the house with snorkel and mask to do some skin-diving in the gulleys. I would not have moved out into that sun if it hadn't been for the prospect of the wet cool sea. I looked back at one point, just before going over the edge of the headland and down to the rocks, and saw the woman, empty-handed and obviously unsuccessful in her search for work, starting up the hill on her way back to Glendore.

That hill, the sun, the long walk. Possibly even a walk that Lena has not yet made . . . but will one day in the time that still lies ahead of her when she walks away with Boesman at the end of the play; a walk beyond the moment of rebellion —— that possibility past, even forgotten —— a walk beyond all the battles, the refusals, even tears. Surrender: Defeat. A walk into the ignominy of silence, the world's silence and blindness, burdened now as never before by Lena's unanswerable little words: Why? How? Who?

And a few years later there was Patience — 'My English name is Patience' — with her baby on her back on the road outside Graaff-Reinet.

ELSA: I nearly didn't stop for her. She didn't signal that she wanted a lift or anything like that. Didn't even look up when I passed . . . I was watching her in the rearview mirror. Maybe that's what told me there was a long walk ahead of her . . . the way she had her head down and just kept on walking. And then the baby on her back. It was hot out there, hot and dry and a lot of empty space . . . There wasn't a farmhouse in sight. She looked very small and unimportant in the middle of all that. Anyway, I stopped and reversed and offered her a lift. Not very graciously. I was in a hurry and wanted to get to the village before it got dark. She got in and after a few miles we started talking. Her English wasn't very good, but when I finally got around to understanding what she was trying to tell me it added up to another typical South African story. Her husband, a farm labourer, had died recently, and no sooner had they buried him when the baas told her to pack up and leave the farm. So there she was . . . on her way to the Cradock district, where she hoped to find a few distant relatives and a place to live. About my age. The baby couldn't have been more than a few months old. All she had with her was one of those plastic shopping bags they put your groceries in at supermarkets. I saw a pair of old slippers. She was barefoot.

So now it is Pumla walking. Was it purposeful? Heading straight to the tracks, her mind made up, very clear about what she was going to do? Holding the hands of her small children, crooning softly to the baby on her back, hoping the infant would stay asleep until the end? No. I reject that scenario. Lying there in the dark it surprises me to realise that even though all I have and know about Pumla Lolwana is her name and those of her children, I now have such a strong sense of her dark presence that I feel I have the authority to accept or reject possible scenarios concerning her. I see instead a random drift through that wasteland of lives called the Samora Machel Informal Settlement in search of something – a friend, or a relative, or the man, husband or boyfriend, who didn't come home with his pay-packet the night before, a search for anything or anybody that could be a source of hope, give her a reason to live. She never found it and when she finally paused to rest, with little Sesanda asking 'Where are we going Mommy? What's wrong Mommy?' she was at the side of the railway tracks and a train was coming.

Women walking. Always women. Is the reason for that as simple as that early childhood memory I have of my mother, possibly the earliest? She was trudging heavily and wearily up the hill to where we lived and I had run to meet her. She was dispirited and depressed after a bad day in the bakery where she worked and it was a terrible shock to see her like that. She was the central and most important presence in my life. Seeing her defeated meant that my whole world was in danger of collapsing. In the years that followed I saw my mother, metaphorically speaking, trudging up that hill many times. Her life was one long struggle for survival – for herself and her family. But she and because of her Lena and Milly and Hester and Miss Helen and all the other women in my work who draw their inspiration from my mother, were never defeated and that is the cardinal difference. Pumla Lolwana was. And it is that difference which maybe now defeats me and makes Pumla Lolwana the dark mystery she will always be for me. There was no hope left.

Lying there in the dark I realise that the freight train has long since passed and all is silent once again, that soft sibilant silence of a sleeping suburban world. I can't even hear the surf which is only a few hundred yards away from where I lie in my bed.

29th June

I read:

> *By Monday night nobody had claimed the bodies of the mother and her*
> *three children from the Salt River mortuary.*

Nobody ever did. Pumla Lolwana's story ends in a sandy wind-
blown cemetery on the Cape Flats where she and her children were
given a pauper's burial. I realise suddenly that there is another
personal connection here, this one going back all of fifty years to
London where my wife Sheila and I are in the Everyman's Cinema
in Hampstead watching The Burmese Harp. It is a beautiful film
with its unforgettable central image of a Japanese Buddhist monk
travelling through a war-ravaged Burmese landscape burying the
bodies of fellow countrymen killed in battle and left to rot on the
battlefields. At the time I didn't appreciate how deep an impression this film had made on me. I certainly recognised it as a deeply
religious work of art but that is as far as it went. Now I see it as
possibly the genesis of a theme – burying the dead – which has
been there in my work from fairly early on and very much so in
recent years. The story of Antigone captured my imagination at an
very early age. It is hard to think of a story that could have been
more urgently needed in the Apartheid South Africa in which I
grew up than that of the young girl defying the laws of the state
because the unwritten laws of her conscience demanded that she
bury her brother. It was inevitable that sooner or later Serpent
Players – the Black drama group I started in Port Elizabeth –
would take on Sophocles' magnificent play. The story of that one
lone voice raised in protest against what she considered an unjust
law struck to the heart of every member of the group. This
production had long-term consequences, leading to the arrest of a
member of the group who then staged a two-character version of
the play – just Creon and Antigone – on Robben Island which in
turn led eventually to the writing of The Island. Some years later a

photograph of two South African soldiers dumping the bodies of dead Swapo fighters in a mass grave in South West Africa lead to the writing of Playland. A few years after that a newspaper item about unclaimed bodies in a police mortuary in the then Transvaal – victims of a Black-on-Black political massacre – resulted in the story of Lukas Jantjies, a Coloured man just a few years older than myself who is haunted by the thought of those unclaimed bodies. And now those of Pumla Lolwana and her three children in the Salt River mortuary. Is that what hooked me when I first read the story? Was that possibly the reason why I couldn't pass it over, consign to oblivion as in fact time is trying to do to it? Is that why she has haunted me? Must I claim her? Yes, I want to do that. As I sit at my table this morning the deepest impulse in my heart is to claim them as mine. And why not! Nobody else wanted them. Maybe that is what I've been trying to do these past weeks at this table, claim her and her children and bury them in the blank pages of this notebook. With that thought I feel that something has changed inside me in much the same way as the haunting stopped for Lukas Jantjies when he realised he had to bury the dead.

Every Sunday night here in southern California I drive inland for two hours to Metta – a Thai Buddhist Forest Monastery in an isolated valley to join the Abbot and his five monks for the evening chanting and meditation. I centre my very simple Buddhist practice around one section of the chanting:

All human beings are the owners of their actions, heir to their actions, born of their actions, related through their actions and live dependent on their actions.

Whatever they do, for good or for evil, to that will they fall heir.

On my last visit I told the Abbot about Pumla Lolwana and her children and asked him if there was a prayer I could say or something I could do for the four of them. He suggested that I should dedicate whatever merit I earned from my next meditation, to them. How do I do that, I asked? Say it, he said. Simply say aloud or to yourself 'I dedicate whatever merit ...'

I started by saying their names aloud, because apart from a few impersonal facts, that is all I have of them:

Pumla Lolwana ... 35 years old

Sesanda Lolwana ... 5 years old

Andile Lolwana ... 3 years old

Lindani Lolwana ... 2 years old

Those four names have become infinitely precious to me. For all I know, here where I am, ten thousand miles away from where they died, I might be the only person left still thinking and saying them. They tell their own story – starting with those of the two boys, a simple story that's speaks of a family that had grown stronger with each of their births; then came little Lindani, the daughter the mother had prayed and waited for. And then of course the mother herself: Pumla ... which in Xhosa means to rest, to sleep, to find peace.

I was wrong when I started out to think that I needed to 'understand' what happened that Friday afternoon on the tracks between Philippi and Nyanga. That isn't why Pumla Lolwana stopped my life. It wasn't either to witness – that thin newspaper report did all that could be done by those who weren't there, didn't see it. I had to claim her, for myself. Now, having done that I have a sense as powerful as the one that made me stop a few weeks ago, that I can move on.

30th June

I ended the day with a sunset walk next to the tracks. It was a quiet one. No trains passed. In spite of a very dry season the Statice are still putting on a show. Out at sea there were a few distant pools of silvery light when sunshine has broken through a bank of cloud and spilt onto the water. Also, a cool and very refreshing breeze. I looked at my wrist watch: 8pm here, 4am in the morning in Cape Town. When I got back to my table I went

online to get Cape Town's weather forecast: it promised a cloud-
less, sunny day with light winds and a maximum temperature of
19 °C. The people of the Samora Machel Squatter Camp were in
for a beautiful, mild winter's day — another three hours of darkness before sunrise.

To Whom It Must Concern

ROELF VISAGIE

My name is Roelf Visagie. I am thirty-five years old. I was the driver of the train that you read about in the newspaper – the one that killed the woman and her baby there on the other side of Redhouse. But I'll tell you all about that later. Here I just want to say I know what I am doing. I'm telling you that because I also know what people are saying about me, that I'm crazy and things like that, but I am not. I am also not drunk. I can't even remember when was my last drink. And just in case you are wondering about that as well, I don't smoke dagga. I am doing what I am doing because I have to do it. So don't ask me things like when am I going back to Lorraine and Danny and Prissy and what about my job, because I don't know. For the moment I am here in Shukuma which is a part of Motherwell and I know it is right. Simon says there is a good chance that the Ama-gintsa (that is what he calls the Tsotsis) don't like it that a White man is living here in their world and that they say they are going to get me.

When you think about it that makes sense in a funny sort of way doesn't it, especially if this is where she came from. I can certainly see they don't like me here and I don't blame them for that but I am trying to make friends with them so we must just wait and see what happens. I am writing all this down because I want to talk to you, you the person who is reading this. I want to tell you what happened. That way you will know the whole story and maybe understand. Because apart from old Simon nobody else does. I'm not exaggerating. I've tried them all. My family, my friends, the officials, and I can see by the way they look at me what they are thinking — he's crazy. So hear me out. That's all I ask. I want one of my own people to hear me out.

Let me start off by saying that I am not trying anymore to find out who she was, you know her name and all that. It's hopeless. Believe me I have tried everything. I have made enquiries at my head office, at the police station, the one here in Motherwell and also the one in Swartkops, and they all looked at me as if to say 'Why are you wasting our time with this?' I am not exaggerating. They simply don't care. But I shouldn't be surprised at that because to tell you the truth it was the same with me at first. No, let me get this straight. I thought I didn't. Because I only started trying to find out her name after I had smashed up the Christmas tree.

Before that she was just some woman from the bush. I think those were my very words when Lorraine asked me about her when I told her what had happened — just some woman from the bush. Because you see it really looked as if I was getting on top of my situation. In the two weeks between the accident and Christmas I had two sessions with Miss Conradie — she's the social worker there at head office to help us if we got problems. I suppose those sessions may have helped a little bit but to be honest with you I don't like talking about my feelings to a strange woman, specially a young one like Miss Conradie even if she has got a certificate from Stellenbosch hanging on her wall. She did do me a favour though by making head office give me sick-leave, so maybe she understood a little bit more than I'm thinking. But if you were just watching me from the outside during those two weeks you would have said that Roelf Visagie is on the mend.

I tried to keep my mind off things by working in the garden, doing Christmas shopping with Lorraine — that is when we bought the Christmas tree — and just anything else you know that would keep my hands busy. I'm one of those guys that if his hands is busy, he's happy. The one thing that should have warned me that things were cooking up inside me, was the nightmares. Even with the pills that the doctor gave me I would still wake up with the fear of hell in my heart man because I was in the cab and she was there on the railway line waiting for me. It was getting so hard on Lorraine, because she had to be at work at Clicks the next day, that I started sleeping on the pull-out sofa in the lounge. It is easy to see now that that was a big mistake because that meant I was right in there with the Christmas tree.

Breaks my heart man when I think about it now. Because we were really all so happy when I put up the tree, and the children decorated it and I switched on the fairy lights. Lorraine and I had tears in our eyes as we played Silent Night on the hi-fi.

It didn't happen that night. It was a few nights later. Same old story. I took the sleeping pill, I fell asleep and then there she was again in front of me and this time there was also crowds of people on the side of the line watching it happen like it was some sort of sport going on. I was frightened in the dream and I was frightened when I was awake because I sort of knew, lying there on the sofa, that she wasn't ever going to go away. So it was once again a case of 'Do something Roelfie. Just get up and do something.'

There was a second box of fairy lights that I hadn't used so I decided to put them on the tree as well. I did that and then switched them all on and sat on the sofa looking at them blinking on and off and on and off. If you were sitting here with me now in this pondok you would see me shaking my head because that is what I am doing as the memory comes back. It was like a fucking bomb exploding inside me man. Or a wild animal that escapes from its cage and just wants to kill anything in front of it, anything it sees. And for me it was that stupid bloody Christmas tree blinking on and off and on and off. So I smashed it. Finish and klaar. I ripped the lights out of the wall like they was its roots and I picked up the tree and started smashing it on the floor and when I was finished there they were standing in the doorway, looking at me with frightened eyes. Lorraine and the kids. She was holding on to them as if I was going to smash them on the floor as well.

All I could think of to say was 'What the fucking hell are you all staring at?'. And Lorraine said 'These are your children Roelf Visagie – go swear at your woman from the bush.' Then she took the kids into the bedroom and I could hear her lock the door. I heard her say to them, 'Your father's gone mad.' But there you have it: 'Go swear at your woman from the bush.' One day I must tell Lorraine what a big favour she did me when she said that.

When I heard those words it was like something just opened up inside me because I suddenly realised you see that that is what I wanted to do! Ja! I wanted to take a deep breath and then load up my lungs with every dirty thing I had ever heard – and I am not just talking about jou ma se moer because believe me I can do a lot better than that – and then say them into the face of that woman who still stands there waiting for me in my dreams. I wanted those to be the last words she hears when my train hits her. Can you understand that? Look at what she did to my life for God's sakes. If she wanted so much to kill herself why didn't she just take her baby and jump into the river. That would have done it. Why did she have to drag someone else – ME! – into her nonsense.

But the trouble was I didn't know her name! I mean you know how it is don't you. When you talk to somebody in your mind you think their name don't you? You don't just say 'Hey you this' and 'Hey you that'. And that is how the ball started rolling. There in the lounge, with Lorraine and the kids hiding away from me in the bedroom, standing there with the pieces of the Christmas tree lying around me, I suddenly had this wonderful feeling that if I could get her name and swear at her properly, just once vloek and skel her out in English and in Afrikaans – because I'm fully bilingual – I would be all right. I know that sounds stupid now, but I'm telling you the truth man. I just wanted to swear at her properly.

That's how it started. But listen ... My hand is starting to get the cramps so I am going to stop now. The last time I tried to write something as long as this was in school – PE Technical College. And anyway I also don't know how long this ballpoint is going to last so I'm going to get a new one just in case.

———◄ O ►———

So here we go again. Now – you would think that finding out the name of a dead person was a straightforward matter wouldn't you. Well think again my friend. How long is it now since Christmas? Two months? Or is it three? Whatever it is here I sit in Shukuma and I still don't know who she was. You get that? I still don't know her name! So when I tell you that I'm not trying to find out who she was anymore, don't think it was because I didn't try. The very next morning after I smashed up the Christmas tree I did what any sensible person would do – I went to the Swartkops Police Station because they handled the matter. A Sergeant Boezak was in charge of the case. Short little arse and very full of himself – you could sommer see that from the way his badge and his boots was shining – so I thought he was going to give me a hard time but when I told him who I was he softened up immediately. So I told him that all I wanted was to know who she was. He just shook his head. 'Mr Visagie,' he said, 'forget it. She's gone into the books as name unknown.' He explained that what he called the procedure was to wait for somebody to come and report a missing person. In her case nobody had come.

So I asked him if they had also made enquiries on their side and he said no that was not part of the procedure and why was I so eager to know her name. So I told him what had happened at home and that all the fucking Christmas trees in Port Elizabeth would be in danger if I didn't find out who she was. He could see I meant business so he said he would make an exception in my case and send one of his constables into the bush where the accident happened to make enquiries. He explained that there were a lot of people squatting in the bush. I asked him if I could go with his constable and he said yes. Trying to find out who she was has led me to some strange places and that bush was the first one. Thorn bush hey! The prickly pears there are so thick that even though I had my jacket on and was always on the footpaths, my arms and legs were scratched to hell at the end of it.

I walked that bush high and low three times – one time with that Black policeman from the Police Station and two times by myself. From one miserable bloody pondok to another. And every time I asked them: 'Is anybody here missing a woman and a baby?' Sometimes they would ask: 'What did she look like?' ... and I would tell them: 'She was a young woman. Red doek on her head, an old bluish coloured dress, barefoot and a grey blanket that was holding the baby on her back.' I knew that description off by heart. Then of course they would just shake their heads and sometimes I could see they wasn't even listening to me. A couple of times they hated me very much and then it was 'Suga wena' or 'Voetsek Whiteman' which was okay because I wanted to say: 'And you fuck-off as well', and I did.

One fellow was drunk and asked me if I wanted to fuck a Black woman and said he would get me one. It's pathetic man! Those people live like animals. No lavatories so their places was always stinking of shit if you don't mind me saying so – the children crawling around in the dirt with no clothes on. I told one women to wipe her baby's nose because he was eating his own snot. What made it worse is that I got so deurmekaar on those footpaths I would end up at the same pondok two or three times and start asking my questions until they would say 'Why is the Baas asking us again?' It was too much for me man. I'm telling you that if I was forced to live like that I would also rather put my baby on my back and go and stand on the line and wait for the next train to Uitenhage.

After those three days in the bush I was the one who was saying to myself 'What's the matter with you Roelf Visagie! Have you gone crazy or something? It's over and done with man. She's dead and gone. And it wasn't your fault. Get back to your life.'

And I tried. I went back home and scrubbed myself under the shower until I was pink to get the smell of that bush and those pondoks out of me and then went out and bought an even bigger Christmas tree than the one I had smashed up. And also fairy lights and all sorts of shit to hang on the branches. The children loved it so for a little while so that sort of made things easy again at home though of course Lorraine couldn't help telling us that we were wasting our time decorating the tree because Christmas was already past. She was really pissed off with me so to try and make her also happy I went fishing with Des one night because Lorraine just loves fresh Grunter but I didn't catch anything and I also had another session with Miss Conradie. Because I was now really trying to turn over a new page as they say. I said to myself: 'Fuck it Roelfie, this time really talk to her' because you see I hadn't really opened up to her on the other times. Anyway I decided I would do so this time.

When I think about it now I don't know that that was such a good idea. When I told her about how I smashed the Christmas tree and then the dream that I was lost on the footpaths in the prickly pear bush and how they was all decorated with fairy lights and glitter ... I shake my head and laugh at it now but so would you if you had seen the look on that dolly's face when I told her all that. 'You smashed the Christmas tree?' she asked me like I had told her that I threw my old mother in the Swartkops River. 'Yes,' I said 'I smashed it to smithereens.' And laughed. She didn't. So I tried to explain to her that it was all because I didn't know the woman's name. I had enough sense not to tell Miss Conradie that I wanted the name so that I could swear at her.

To tell you the truth I don't even know if I wanted to swear at her anymore. By now it was more like I just wanted to be able to say her name, say Dora, or Maria, or Sophie or whatever the hell it was when she stood there in front of me again. Maybe then in my dream she would say something back to me. Who knows? Dreams is dreams man and anything can happen in them. And to tell you the truth I didn't even need a dream to try it out. If I was sitting somewhere quiet I could actually try out some names on her, you know imagine myself talking to her and waiting for her to say something.

Ja, that is how real it was. She wasn't even on the railway lines anymore, she was there in front of me, alive, ready to say something if I could just get the right name. But to cut a long story short it was a case of 'Goodbye Miss Conradie and thanks for nothing and hello there Sergeant Boezak' because I went back to the Swartkops Police Station. I just wanted to check up in case he had discovered something in the meantime. He hadn't of course but he did say he had been thinking about it and his guess now was that maybe she had come from Motherwell because that was also where a lot of the prickly pear sellers came from. He told me to go straight to the Police Station and make my enquiries there.

So, off we go to Motherwell. I've got a lot to say about this place but I'll do that later. That first time I didn't see much because I did what Boezak said and went straight to the Police Station. They were a real hard-arsed lot in that charge office — made Boezak at Swartkops look like a gentleman. I mean she was a Black woman for Christ's sake — one of them. But no — they weren't going to do a damn thing to help a White man even if it was for one of their own kind. Just no respect for the living or the dead. All I could get out of them was that they had plenty of missing people in their books but no young woman in a blue dress with a red doek and a baby on her back. They said I should try the Police Morgue — the place where they keep the dead bodies from accidents and murders and that sort of thing. Go there they said to me and see if anyone has come there to identify her. It's really funny you know. When I got into my car and drove out of that hell-hole I promised myself that I would never be back but guess what — here I am sitting in one of the bloody pondoks writing to you! Life is strange. Anyway I got cramps again so I'm taking a rest

———————⪦○⪧———————

I see I was telling you about the Morgue. What maybe you don't
know is that the identification and everything is all done by a
book — or maybe I should say by many books. Sounds crazy I
know but I'm not joking. The Morgue is part of the Police
Station up there on the hill near the Hospital. The guy in charge
up there was a regular old-style Afrikaner and what a relief it was
to be talking to one of my own people for a change. His name was
Van Deventer. I introduced myself and when I told him why I was
there I could see he really wanted to help me. He asked me for the
date of the accident and then took me inside to a little room with
a table and some chairs and told me to wait. He went away and
then came back with a big book which he said was for the date I
had given him. You'll find her in there he said. That was how the
identification process worked. Can you believe it? I opened the
book and there they were, pictures of their faces — one straight on
and one from the side — and next to the pictures what old Van
Deventer called 'the relevant detail'. You know, the date and so on.
All of them non-Whites. I was supposed to turn over the pages
and look through the book until I found her.

So now I must tell you something strange. As I turned the pages
and looked at the pictures — men and women, young, old, some of
them with blood and bruises on the faces, eyes open, eyes closed —
as I was looking at them and turning the pages I suddenly realised
that I couldn't remember anymore what she looked like! It's true.
She was clean out of my mind. Van Deventer was standing watching me and when he saw that I had stopped turning the pages he
asked me if I had found her. I told him No and explained to him
what the trouble was — that all the faces in the book were now in
my head with her and I couldn't tell which was which. He said that
in that case he couldn't help me. He closed the book and took it

away. I could see he wanted me to leave but I was feeling very weak and just sat there for a few minutes and then got up and left.

There was like a little park on the other side of the street outside with some benches so I crossed over and went and sat down on one of them. I wanted to cry man. I've never been so lonely in all my life. There were some Black nannies with babies near by and because I didn't want them to see me cry I closed my eyes like I was enjoying the sunshine but I was crying. And then suddenly there she was again in front of me, standing on the railway lines, waiting for me. The eyes, the nose, the mouth, the red doek on her head – everything as clear as a photograph in Van Deventer's book. I hurried back inside the Morgue, made him get the book again, and this time I found her. I was even more frightened this second time when I turned the pages because I thought that maybe her face would be all smashed up. You see I didn't look when they pulled her out from under the coach. I had gone into the bush to be sick. But it wasn't. She was looking back at me on that page just the way she had done on the railway line. That's her I said, pointing to the picture. That is definitely her. And I was laughing man and just so happy because I had found her. Now you tell me what that is all about. This woman from the bush with a baby on her back who is making a mess of my whole life and is now also dead mark you, makes me happy the way I was when little Prissy was born. Can you explain that to me?

Anyway, I had found her and I swore to myself that I would never forget her face again ever. And it's true. I can close my eyes anytime, anywhere, and there she is. But you know what? She was still unidentified! Yes. Nobody had come and claimed her. 'So what happened?' I asked Van Deventer? 'Have you still got her here?' 'Good Heavens no,' Van Deventer said. 'We can't keep them here forever man. This isn't a boarding house. Her time was up so she got a pauper's burial. Motherwell cemetery. That's where you'll find her – but remember to take a spade with you. Ha! Ha!'

I just looked at him. I just looked at him because believe me if he wasn't an old man I would have said something. I wasn't in any mood for jokes, specially not about her. When he stopped laughing he looked at me and asked, 'What is it all about Visagie? You and her. Why are you trying to find her? She's dead and buried my friend.' I couldn't believe he was asking me that because I mean I had told him. So I told him again. 'Don't you understand?' I said. 'It's because I killed her man. She's mine. She's all I got now and I don't know who the fuck she is. Okay? Is it so fucking hard to understand that? What the hell is the matter with all you people!' Van Deventer just stood there staring at me and shaking his head. I could see he didn't understand. Anyway we shook hands, I thanked him for his help and then I left. So there you got it – as they used to say in school – 500 words about my visit to the Morgue.

I had to go and walk around after that last session. Telling you about Van Deventer got me all worked up again because I'm not really like that. I don't like swearing. Specially not at an old man. But seriously now, why is it that people find it so hard to understand? Do you? If you was sitting here in this pondok with me would you also stare at me like him, like Des, like my wife Lorraine, and shake your head? What would you say? Because that is what they all did, shake their heads and look the other way. I mean I can still in a kind of way understand Van Deventer or Miss Conradie. They don't know me. They don't know what I am really like. But Des? We've been pals for I don't know how long man. He knows me like a brother would. He knows I'm the one who is always fetching the moer-stok and putting the fish out of their misery when they jump around on the bank because I don't like to see living things suffer. I'm the one who throws the sand sharks back into the water. Or when I am driving along, even if it's just a little mossie that flies into my windscreen I get sick in the stomach. And Des knew that. I mean damn it all he had seen it with his own eyes. But then that night when we went fishing – when I told him about the woman and the baby and how I can't find out who she was there he is also looking at me the way Van Deventer did. Like I'm crazy or something.

And it wasn't like I didn't try to explain it to him. I don't know exactly where the Bible says it but somewhere in the black book it says you mustn't kill. And this wasn't a mossie or a sand shark for God's sake. It was a woman with a baby on her back. But the one that hurts me most man is my nearest and dearest – my own family. Lorraine and Danny and Prissy. You know if I was one of those drunk buggers who come home on a Friday night with a half empty pay packet and swear at everybody and carry on until the police got to come and shut him up, then yes. Then look at me anyway you like. But I'm not one of them. Sure I like my drinks, but then so does Lorraine. When the kids are asleep we both like a couple of drinks to get things going between us. And I never drink at work. I've looked after every job I've had. Go ask Miss Conradie to show you my work sheets if you don't believe me. The system manager himself has congratulated me personally. We were a happy family man. In the week after the accident even though I was a bloody mess inside I forced myself to go shopping with Lorraine for the Christmas presents for the kids. Do you know what that was like for me? Have you got any fucking idea what it was like to have Father Christmas with his cotton wool beard ringing his bell in your face and asking for money for the Salvation Army when you've still got the smell of that woman's shit in your nose because that's what you smelt when you got out of the cab to see her legs sticking out under the first coach. No! Time for another walk. I'll pick up when I come back.

So I was telling you about Lorraine and me. I am going to start off by saying again that it was a happy marriage. What's the matter with me! IS a happy marriage because I will be back with her and Danny and Prissy when this is all over. I'll make it up to them. I know she has said she doesn't want to see me anymore because she believes I'm spending my time fucking Black women but I can swear for you on a Bible that I am not. I'll even get a doctor's certificate to prove to her that I haven't got Aids. After all every marriage has its up and downs not so? And ours was no different. But fifteen years and two lovely children says something doesn't it? After all that's the important consideration – the children.

Now I must be honest with you about one thing. With the two of us – me and Lorraine – it wasn't a case of love at first sight. In fact if someone had shown me her picture before I met her I would have said that no ways was that woman going to be Mrs Roelf Visagie. When I told her that for a joke one day she said it was the same for her when she saw me the first time. That is what I respect about her. Honesty. And that's the way it has been all through our marriage. We've discussed everything with no holds barred. Now tell me truthfully, after fifteen years of a marriage like that wouldn't you also be expecting a little understanding? A little patience. I mean fucking hell it wasn't like it was every day that I came home and said 'I killed a woman today'. And then after I told her what happened – what's the first thing she says? 'Does that mean you're going to lose your job?'

Of course I can maybe understand her worrying about that but when she then goes on about it – my job this, my job that – every bloody day while I'm trying to get a hold of myself?

Alright, so I shouldn't have lost my temper and smashed up the Christmas tree, but truly man I couldn't help it. There she is standing with the kids when I switched on the fairy lights and Silent Night is playing on the hi-fi and she says 'Enjoy it children because there won't be one next year if your father loses his job.' Nice way to put us all in the Christmas spirit, hey? The only other idea that Lorraine seemed to have in her head was that the woman was drunk – as if that would have made any difference. 'Did they smell her breath?' she asks me. 'How do you smell the breath of a dead person?' I ask her. 'What about a blood test?' she asks me. 'I don't know,' I say. 'Then ask them to do one,' she says. 'I don't think it makes any bloody difference,' I say, 'whether she was drunk or sober.' 'Yes it will,' she says 'because then you won't lose your job.' And off she goes again about my job. It was bad enough being so the hell in with her that I wanted to smash a lot more than just the Christmas tree.

But then I also started feeling guilty because I could see how much I was hurting her and the kids. That started one night when the pills the doctor gave me and the brandy knocked me out. I was still sleeping in the bed with her that time. I managed to sleep for a little bit and then I woke up. I knew something was going on but it took me a few minutes to realise what it was because the pills and the brandy was still making me giddy. Lorraine was crying. You got to know what that means man. In all the time we was married I saw her cry maybe three times that I can remember ... but it was always happiness that did it. Not this time. Believe me there was no happiness between the two of us in that bed that night. What made it worse is that she was trying her hardest to keep it quiet. It was awful man. I just lay there listening to her little crying sounds hating myself for what I was doing to her. Hating that Black woman for what she was doing to us. After a few minutes I tried to make it up with Lorraine. I said her name and touched her but she just rolled on her side with her back to me and stopped crying. Nothing more.

Awful man! And don't think the kids didn't know what was going on. I told them about the accident the very same day it happened but it was the trouble between me and Lorraine that really frightened them. And then also the smashing of the Christmas tree. That was the finishing touch alright. I am really ashamed about that now. So I'm feeling ashamed, I'm feeling guilty, I'm pissed off with the whole world and you are now maybe also asking Why? Not so? Why do you keep on Roelf Visagie? Why don't you just leave this place where you don't belong and go back to them and say you're sorry and start your life again. Fair enough my friend – so you have now had your say and I have heard you. My turn now so please let me have my say and you listen. I can't. Simple as that. I'm on the rails you see and there is only one way to go – forward. There's no going back, there's no turning left, there's no turning right. That was the hell of it you see. Being there in the cab, seeing her step out onto the rails and stand there waiting for me with me knowing there was nothing I could do to stop what was going to happen. That's the joke you see. They talk about the driver 'being at the controls' but there is quite simply no fucking control. Not then when I was sitting there in the cab. Not now when I am sitting here in this pondok. The only difference is that this time I don't know who or what is waiting for me. All I can do is wait for whatever is waiting for me. After that maybe I'll be able to get out of this pondok the way I got out of that cab and go back home. Do you understand now?

But just before I leave off this time I want to tell you something funny. I've been writing to you all this time thinking you were a man. But hey, suppose you're a woman? What then? Well I suppose I must watch my language in future if that is the case. But now comes something even funnier – you ready for it? – suppose you are Black? I mean why not. If Roelf Visagie can find himself sitting in a pondok in a Motherwell squatter camp writing this, why can't a Black man be sitting somewhere in a nice big house reading it? There sure is enough of them now in nice big houses these days isn't there. Driving around in their Mercs! But listen, I don't care what you are and I don't want to get into bloody politics with you. The New South Africa has got nothing to do with me being here in this pondok. It's about me and that woman with the baby on her back and I'm telling you now that talking to you has helped me a hell of a lot. I don't know what I would have done without you. So thank you.

It's night-time now. Dark outside and I mean really dark. I don't know why it is like that but the darkness here in Shukuma is thick like I've never seen it anywhere else. If you was here with me and we went outside you would see some big street lights in the distance – sort of floodlights like the ones they switch on for football matches at night. But none of their light reaches here. This is a squatter camp area and the only lights you see here are the cooking fires in the paraffin tins outside the pondoks and the candles and lamps burning inside. This is a world of red fires and smoke that burns your eyes and dark shapes moving around, and there is no way you can know if it's a friend or a skelm coming towards you until it's too late. That is why Simon doesn't want me to go outside at night. He says there are skelms looking for me.

I'm telling you my friend if your Sunday School days didn't give you a picture of hell when you was little then come visit me here one night and you'll get one. Because that is what I thought the first time I walked around here in the dark. 'This is hell Roelfie,' I said to myself. 'This is hell and this is where you belong.' But don't think it is any better in the daylight. If you was to say to me 'Motherwell or Redhouse bush, choose,' I wouldn't have a problem. Redhouse bush any day! It's at least green! And there's prickly pears. This place is grey and there's fuck all nothing except rubbish, rusty iron pondoks and misery. And then of course to get the full picture you must add all the smells to it as well. I am telling you my friend there are smells around here that you haven't even dreamt of. Pondok perfume!

I am writing this in Simon's pondok and I'm waiting for him. He went to the shop to buy us something to eat. Have you ever been inside a pondok? Now's your chance. Step inside my friend and I'll show you around. But be careful of your head hey – the roof is not high enough for you to stand up straight. That corner there on the other side with the old mattress on the pieces of cardboard is where Simon sleeps. That box next to the bed is where he keeps his things. Then comes a little table and two kitchen chairs where I am sitting and writing and behind me is some blankets on the floor where I sleep. No window and one sort of door which hangs crooked. When I want to wash he fetches me a bucket of water from outside somewhere. I've been living here with him for five days now. I know this all looks like madness to you but believe me it isn't. When I first came here I didn't know what the hell was going on but now I do and I think you will agree with me when you have read all I want to say to you. What will surprise you my friend is when I tell you that Simon understands. Ja. This old Outa with his broken teeth and his bad English understands me more than any of the others – not Lorraine, or my children, or Miss Conradie or my best friend Des – none of them understood. But I know Simon does. He can't read this of course but he likes to sit and watch me write it. So don't think he's a fool. He may be an old man but he has seen a lot of life. He knows what the score is. I met him when Mr Mdoda the undertaker took me to the cemetery. He pointed to Simon who was standing there and told me that he was a part-time grave digger and could maybe help me because he earned his living burying unidentified corpses.

You see one of the things Van Deventer told me at the Morgue was that unidentified corpses were handed over to the undertakers for disposal and he gave me Mr Mdoda's address. Then when I went to Mr Mdoda he told me that when they got one of those bodies from the Morgue for disposal they would give it to what he called a freelance digger to bury because there was nobody to pay for a church ceremony or stuff like that. So there we were after Mr Mdoda drove away, just the two of us, Simon and me among the graves. Graves? I suppose I must call them that but really if it wasn't for the crosses on some of them and the dead flowers you would think they were just piles of rubbish. I know that sounds like disrespect for the dead but it's not because I am telling you the truth. It made me sick in my stomach man. I mean it's people's mothers and dearly beloveds who are lying there isn't it?

You know, if you were to ask me what was the saddest day of my life I would say it was that one – walking around there among those piles of sand, looking at the little crosses with names I couldn't pronounce. Hey man! I'm telling you. One of them just had an old jam tin with sea shells in it where the flowers should have been. I suppose they couldn't find any and wanted to put something pretty on the grave. Because let me tell you this is not a world of pretty flowers my friend. And all I could think is that in one of them the woman and her baby was lying. That hit me man! That hit me hard. I mean, even if she was drunk or babalas like Lorraine says she was, even if she has fucked up my life completely, she was a human being, a young woman, a mother with her baby on her back. I've come to know her face like I know my own, or Lorraine's. But which one? Maybe he knows, I thought, because Simon was standing there watching me. Maybe he buried her. That got me a little bit excited. Because you see I felt very near to her. I don't know how it was supposed to happen but it was like I was going to find her grave or something. So I started walking over to Simon to talk to him. When he saw me coming to him he started to walk away and I had to shout at him to stop. But hang on – speak of the devil and here he is. Simon has just come in with our supper. I'll stop now while we eat and then carry on.

Like I said he's sitting there now watching me – I wish you could see him because he is quite something to look at. My guess is that he's old enough to be my father because the hairs of his little beard – and believe me it really is little because you could count the hairs if you wanted to – they are all grey. He's taken his little woollen cap off so I can see that his korrels are also full of grey. His face is very bony and covered with wrinkles. But that doesn't make him ugly. My mother would have called him outa which was her way of saying he was okay and that you could trust him. The only thing you've got to put up with is his very strong smell but to be fair it's not just him. This whole world around here smells like nothing I ever knew before. But I've got used to it now. I suppose I also smell like that now. One other thing about him is that he carries his spade with him wherever he goes.

Let me now go on with how we met. Like I said it was there in the graveyard and because his English and his Afrikaans is not so good that first time I talked with him was very heavy going. In fact I said to myself 'You're wasting your time Roelfie.' So I left him and walked around some more looking at the graves and all the time while I was doing that he just stood there watching me. He was pretending sometimes to be working but I could see he was watching me all the time. I don't know how much time I spent there just walking around. All I can tell you my friend is that at the end of it I was lost. I mean it. I stopped walking and I just stood there in the middle and I didn't know where to go or what to do. I knew of course that I could get back into my car and be back home in twenty minutes but inside it felt like I was a million miles away from my own life, the one I used to have with Lorraine and little Prissy and Danny. I had followed that woman with the red doek and the baby on her back so far away from my world it felt like I would never find my way back to it.

And what made it worse is that I didn't have that feeling anymore that she was near to me. I kept trying to get her back. Every time I looked at another grave I would say to myself 'Maybe this one is hers' and try to bring her back into my mind but there was just so many of them. Sometimes I would see I was standing on one! Or that I had knocked over a cross or an old booze bottle with a plastic flower in it! It was like losing somebody in a crowd only this time all the people in the crowd were dead because I kept seeing the faces in Van Deventer's big book. Every time I looked at a grave it would be one of the faces in the book, but never hers. And I was alone in that crowd. It wasn't me and her anymore. Just me. That did it my friend. That finished me off. Standing there in the middle of all those graves I knew I had come to the end of the road and that it had led me nowhere because I would never know her name.

You see all this time I was thinking that if I knew who she was, if I could say her name the next time she was there in my dream, then she would speak to me. I know that sounds crazy but you got to understand those dreams were real to me. I mean, is it any different me talking to you and telling you everything when I don't know who you are? You see it wasn't a case of wanting to swear at her anymore. That feeling was long gone. What I wanted to do now was tell her who I was. Because when you come to think of it, wasn't she maybe also wondering about me, about my name?

Just stop now and think about it. She's standing there on the railway line and she can see me, she can see the face of the man in the cab driving the train that's going to kill her, doesn't she want to know who I am? Wouldn't you? That's all we got to give each other for fuck's sake. Our names. Why is that so fucking hard to understand? It's just as well I am here in Motherwell and not back home with Lorraine and the kids because if she had said to me one more 'Forget her Roelfie darling' then I would have killed her.

But I was telling you about that day in Boplaas. Like I said I finally know it's useless and I'm sitting there next to the fence with my backside in the dirt and Simon comes over slowly and joins me. I am so fucked up inside I'm not even surprised when he also sits down on the ground on the other side of the fence pole because I'm resting my back against it. Can you imagine it? The two of us sitting there like we were buddies! He was the one who spoke first and this time I could actually understand what he was saying but you'll never guess what it was.

He said there was no White people buried in that graveyard. Do you understand? He thought I was looking for one of my own people. Can you imagine it? In Motherwell cemetery? There's some things you just got to laugh at and another time believe me that is that I would have done. I'm glad I didn't because knowing him now like I do that would have been the end of it between us. Instead I shook my head and said no I wasn't looking for a White person I was looking for a Black person. And because I was so tired I spoke slowly and I said it like I was talking to a child. That did it. That was the start of our communication with each other. Sitting there with the sand and the old plastic bags blowing around us and the crooked little crosses shaking in the wind, I tried to tell him my story.

Now I'll be honest with you – I don't know how much of it he really got, but I know for sure that he understood some things. I got a few Xhosa words like amadoda and that from my mother – she grew up in the Transkei – so when I was telling him about the young woman he shook his head and said he never looks inside. I'm sure he meant the coffins. The important thing though is not really how much he understood but that I know he could feel my feelings. I am ready to swear on a Bible that that is true. Why would he have sat so long next to me there if there wasn't something happening between us? Why would he have sat there shaking his head and speaking softly in his Xhosa language and waving his hand as he looked at all the graves in front of us. And when it started to get dark why did he stand up and look down at me and say 'Come' and bring me back here with him to his pondok. And why did I follow him just like that? Can you tell me the answers? But what I must tell you about now is the dream I had that night in this pondok but I am now wragty too tired to do it now. Tomorrow.

◄○►

This is the dream. It's about the accident. But here is the interesting part. I know it is going to happen and I am standing on the side of the railway line there in the Redhouse bush where I first saw the woman standing, waiting for it to happen. Do you get it? I am OUTSIDE the train, standing there waiting, because I know it is going to happen. But I can't see anything yet – I look down the line towards the bridge but there is no sign of the train and there is also no sign of the woman. But everything else around me is so bright and clear and big, really big man like I was sitting in the front row at the movies. And I go on waiting and still there is no sign of the train or the woman. But now I see something else. I see that I have got a spade just like Simon's in my hand and that makes me very nervous because I know that means that somebody is going to get killed. And then I can also hear the train on the bridge and I am thinking to myself 'You must stop it Roelfie. Go stand there and wave your spade and stop the accident from happening.' And while I am thinking that somebody comes out of the bush but it is very hard for me to see who it is and by now I can also see the train coming but I am just standing there watching because I don't know what to do. But what really frightens me is that when I look carefully I can see that I am driving the train and then the feeling inside me gets worse and worse and then I wake up. That was the dream. So what can I say? What can you say?

This has been one of the most special days in my life and tomorrow I think is going to be even better. Just listen to this. Simon and me were sitting in here talking — he was telling me some long story and I was nodding my head like I understood because it makes me feel good when he talks to me like that — when a little boy comes from Mr Mdoda with a message that he has got work for Simon and that he must be at Boplaas tomorrow because there is two unknowns for him to bury. Simon says okay to the little boy who goes away. I wait for Simon to go on with his story but he just sits there looking at me for a long time. I'm beginning to feel sort of strange with him looking at me like that and I think that maybe he's waiting for me to tell a story about myself so I start looking for one. But then, while I am doing that, he nods his head and — wait for it! — he smiles! I swear to God he smiles or at least that is what I think it is because I have never seen that look on his face since I've known him. I'm getting ready to smile back but then before I can do it he gets up, grabs his spade and goes out which is quite strange because it is already very dark outside. Anyway, I don't know how long he is gone because I am quite happy just sitting there thinking about the stories I got in my life and which one I would like to tell him. I am still busy with that when Simon comes back. I just wish you were here with me so I could see the look of surprise in your eyes when I tell you what I saw. Here it is: Simon is standing there and he has got two spades. Ja, read it again my friend. Two spades. His own and another one and he is looking at me and I know that the other spade is for me because I am going to dig with him tomorrow. He is looking at me and I am looking at him and I nod my head to say yes I understand and he nods his head. Nothing else. He puts the spades down next to his mattress, lies down and goes to sleep.

So there you have it. What can I say to you now? How can I tell you about the feeling I got inside me now as I write this, the feeling that came into me when I understood why Simon had two spades. I don't know how because I don't know what its name is. I've never had this feeling before. All I can tell you for sure is that I know it's going to be alright. Everything. Because that is why I am here in this pondok. I must dig tomorrow with Simon and bury those unknowns. When I've done that I can go back home. Maybe you don't believe me. I don't blame you. There's a part of me also that is saying 'What the hell is going on with you Roelf Visagie?' But I just smile and shake my head because everything is going to be alright. I'll speak to you once more tomorrow night and tell you what it was like. I think that will be the last time we talk.

I'm going out for a walk now.

MISS ESTELLE CONRADIE

What a terrible business! First the woman and the baby and then him. The more I think about it now that it is all over the more I ask myself: Why? Yes! – I know I should be satisfied with the psychological and sociological explanations for what happened because after all I spent four years at university learning them and they of course do make sense. I mean it doesn't take much imagination to understand why the woman did what she did. Her story looks to me like the classic one of desperation born, as they say, out of poverty and heaven knows what all, because when you come to think of it some of those Black people do have it very hard. Even though I haven't got any children of my own as yet I can imagine what it must be like to have a hungry baby crying all day for something to eat when there is no food in the house or money to buy it. But Visagie? He had everything going for him. A healthy young man with a wife and two lovely children, a good job with medical aid and prospects. Because as far as we were concerned he was one of our best drivers – never missed a day's work from illness, his paperwork always up to date. But then he goes and throws it all away! Severe depression? Of course, but is that enough? I had a very religious upbringing you know so there's a part of me that can't stop there and still has to ask: Why? Why in heaven's name? And he is not the only one you know. Open your newspaper any day of the week and you'll find other stories like that – men going mad, killing themselves, killing their families and other strange things. It really makes you wonder what is happening to us as a people. Sometimes it really looks to me as if something has gone wrong with the male animal of the Afrikaner species.

But listen, before we go any further let me just warn you I will be talking to you in strict confidentiality. Nothing of what I tell you is for publication. It's the same as with a doctor: a patient's business and problems is strictly private. The drivers and other workers come to me and tell me things because they know their secrets are safe. There are of course certain things I am freely at liberty to say to you and the first one is that you mustn't let this tragedy give you the wrong idea about how things are over here. They are not nearly as bad as in Cape Town or up north on the reef. I was reading in a report just the other day that last month alone there was no less than ten deaths by suicide on the Khayelitsha-Cape Town line alone. I don't have any figures for Johannesburg but heaven alone knows what is going on up there!

Now don't get me wrong and go and say that I was belittling the poor woman. I mean – heavens above! Even if she was the only suicide ever it would still be a terrible tragedy, not so? Oh yes. Definitely suicide! No question about it at all. Visagie said in his report and in his sessions with me that when he first saw her she was standing out of harm's way on the side of the line and that only when there was no chance of him stopping the train in time did she step out onto the rails and face him, stand there waiting for him. And that was in broad daylight mind you. Now if that isn't taking your own life then I would like very much to know what is.

But to get back to Mr Visagie, we had three sessions in all. After the first two it really looked to me like he had got over the trauma of the experience. There was absolutely nothing to alert me to what was coming. In fact there was very nearly nothing at all in those first two sessions because getting Roelf Visagie to talk about his feelings was like trying to squeeze water out of a stone. You know if there is one thing my professors at Stellenbosch drilled into me was that the art of this business is listening. But that is not so easy you know when there is nothing to listen to. I tried everything I could, but like I said getting him to talk needed a miracle. It was of course a very different story with the last session but I'll get to that later.

Those first two visits were in the two weeks between the accident and Christmas and after the second one it looked as if Visagie was recovered and would be back on the job in another week or so. But then in the week after Christmas, Mrs Visagie came in and told me about what he did to the Christmas tree. I realised that that was a warning signal and I told her to tell him to come in and see me again. I see here in his file that that session, which was also his last one with me, took place on January 4th. That session was quite simply the hardest one I have had so far in my career and all because I couldn't give him the woman's name! But please, you mustn't think I didn't understand what he was going through. Or sympathise with him. That is my job. And anyway what he was asking was perfectly normal not so? He wanted to know who he had killed. Anybody would wouldn't they? He had made a few enquiries on his side but when nobody could tell him who she was he asked me to help him. That was I think on his second visit – yes, here it is – the second visit: Request from Mr Visagie to make enquiries concerning the woman's identity.

So I tried, but the truth is I also had no luck. I asked the system manager's office again and again and always the same: 'We are waiting for the docket from the Swartkops police station.' So I eventually phoned the police station and what's the answer? 'The docket is on its way to the system manager's office.' And so it went on for I don't know how long. When eventually the docket did turn up, what do you think? No name! When I told him that, I'm telling you – it was like lighting one of your Big Bangs on Guy Fawkes night. You know, the little sparks as it goes quietly along the wick and then when it is just about to reach the big cracker you hold your breath and stick your fingers in your ears. Well, that is what I felt like doing at the end of that session. It had started off nice and quietly like the other sessions – in fact I remember very clearly that when it looked like there was no hope of getting the woman's name I thought he was just going to laugh it off as another joke about bureaucrats. Because that is what he did to start with. Quietly you know, more like a little chuckle than a big belly laugh, while he kept on saying 'No Name!' like it was some sort of joke.

Then he asks me 'So is it now like they say, "Case Closed"?' He was sitting there where you are, looking at me — he had beautiful big brown eyes — waiting. And you know something? I was almost too scared to tell him: 'Yes, case closed.' Because by then I had already learnt to spot the signs that he was getting worked up again inside. That is the way it was with him. He would always come in very calm but no matter how hard I tried to steer the conversation in the right direction something I said would always light the wick of his big bang. I've been in this job four years now and in that time I've tried to help about ten drivers after they've had accidents on the line and none of them gave me any trouble so to speak. I was fully expecting it to be harder with Mr Visagie because he was the youngest of our drivers and didn't have all that much experience you see. And we mustn't forget that that poor little baby on the woman's back. Can you imagine what it must be like to have that on your conscience as well?

But anyway, after his first session with me when I made my notes as I always do — yes here it is — I wrote: Quiet and coopera-tive — at first very reluctant to talk but by the end of the session he was starting to open up. That is very important you see — getting them to talk about it — and the sooner the better. So there you have it. Quiet and cooperative. I couldn't have been more wrong. From the second session on, every one of them ended up with me wanting to pull out my hair with frustration.

What I learnt very quickly was that Mr Visagie could take anything I said — anything — no matter how ordinary or matter of fact it was, and turn it into an excuse for one of his — I don't know what to call them — outbursts. And once he'd got going there was nothing I could do to stop him so that we could have a proper talk. I tried to make notes the first few times, but I had to give up. I just couldn't keep up with him. It might have been something I said about the weather that day that started him off but by the end of it I was listening to absolute madness about how the government was spending their money on guns and bombs and driving around in big motorcars and doing nothing for the poor people. And if it wasn't the government, then it was God, or his mother-in-law or the whole Afrikaner nation. He would drag in anything and everything and stir it all up and make a potjie-kos of everything that is wrong with the world. I should have made a tape recording of one of them because nobody can really know what it was like from me just telling them about it. I can remember the first time it happened I made a little note 'angry' when he started talking, but at the end of that session I crossed it out and wrote 'rage'. You know the way they speak now about 'road-rage'. Well, believe me that as far as I am concerned there is now also something called 'train-rage' and I know what I'm talking about because I had it here with me in this very office. The thought of that man driving a train gave me goosebumps.

Anyway, at the end of that session I persuaded him to make another appointment – which I was dreading – for him to see me again in two weeks' time, and I also made another appointment for him to see the doctor to ask for stronger sleeping pills. But then of course Mrs Visagie came in and told me about the Christmas tree and I asked for him to come in and see me immediately. That session ended on a really bad note. We didn't even make an appointment for another one. And even if we had I'm The Man who stormed out of this office had no intention of wasting anymore time with 'fat cats behind wooden desks' as he put it.

That is as much as I can tell you. But like everybody else of course I got plenty of questions on my side about this whole business. I mean to start with can you tell me what was he doing in that squatter camp? The report in the newspaper said he had been living there for several days in one of the pondoks. Doesn't that strike you as just a little bit strange? I mean we are talking about a White man and an Afrikaner at that with a wife and two children and a very nice little home of his own. Mrs Visagie told me she was going out of her mind wondering where he was and what he was doing. And talking about that, they are the ones who really suffer not so? Mrs Visagie and her two children. I believe he at least had the decency to leave her some sort of farewell letter which the police found in the pondok and gave to her but I have no idea what was in it. But there again you see, that is almost like he knew what was going to happen to him which only adds to the mystery doesn't it. Speaking confidentially to me, the Station Commander at Motherwell said there was five stab wounds on his body.

So there you have it. To use the words which got him so the hell in during that last session, it is now well and truly 'Case Closed'.

WARRANT OFFICER VICTOR BOEZAK

No name. That's right. No ID book. Nothing! There was one twenty-cent coin in the pocket of her dress and also a paraffin tin with a few prickly pears in it on the side of the railway line, but I can't even tell you for sure that that was hers. But other than that – nothing. Not a single thing you could call a clue for us to work on. You'd be surprised how small the clue can be sometimes that solves the case. I once built up a positive ID of a hit-and-run victim – an old man. Danie Gerritz – I'll never forget his name. All I had to start with was an old bus ticket in one of his jacket pockets. I was stationed at Kareedouw in the Long Kloof at the time. Hit and run. The old fellow had been flattened by some bastard when he was walking along the main road at night. We never caught the culprit but thanks to that bus ticket I was able to trace Danie all the way back to Gelvandale and establish his ID.

But to get back to the young woman. I can't even tell you for sure whether she was an African or a Coloured. The railway guys put her down as Coloured in their report but Constable Ntloko says they are wrong, that she was Black. 'My people' he said. I reckon he should know. In his report the District Surgeon put down their ages as being about twenty-five for the woman and the baby girl as maybe approximately about one year old. Ja, it was a little girl baby. Both of them killed instantaneously on impact. Because it was a fatal accident Visagie had to have an examination as well but everything was normal as far as he was concerned. No trace of alcohol in his blood. Which leaves only one conclusion of course: suicide. Now I didn't see the bodies myself but Ntloko says they looked to be quite healthy and well fed. So then you have to ask why did she do it. Well your guess is as good as mine. I don't mean to be crude but truly I think it's a question of take your pick because there are a hell of a lot of sad stories out there. My guess is desertion. Wife and child was too much for the man so he buggered off.

But coming back to the question of identification because that is what this case was finally all about. Believe me we tried everything. As I explained to Mr Visagie there is a standard procedure to be followed in these cases and we did exactly what was laid down by the rules. But he just wouldn't leave us alone. We had him back here in the Charge Office I don't know how many times asking if we had identified her yet. I felt sorry for the poor man because I could see he was in a bad way. You know, very worked up about it all. Just between you and me I did even more than was laid down in the rules for these cases. To try and put his mind at ease I even sent Constable Ntloko into the bush to make enquiries. There's a lot of squatting going on around there where it happened, specially this time of the year when the prickly pears get ripe. That's the only way some of them have got to earn a few pennies. And do you know what? Mr Visagie went with him! Ja. Ntloko said they spent the whole day walking those footpaths from one little pondok to the other but no luck. Nobody was missing a wife and baby, or a sister or a daughter.

My guess now is that maybe she came from Motherwell. It's not all that far from the scene of the accident and you know those people can walk for miles and think nothing about it. I made the mistake of saying that to Mr Visagie so he was all ready right then to jump into his car with Ntloko and drive there and start making enquiries. Ja! He was already on his way out of the Charge Office when I shouted 'Hokaai Mr Visagie!' to get him back. I pointed out that Motherwell wasn't part of our area so Ntloko had no right to be making enquiries there. That didn't stop him of course but he also got nowhere with them. Looking for somebody in Motherwell without an ID or a name or something to go by is now wragty a case of the needle in the haystack as they say. If you think looking for that needle in the Uitenhage bush is bad, wait until you try finding it in Motherwell. I was stationed there in '98 and it was bad enough then. But now! I had to take some dockets over there last month and get a couple of statements from witnesses for another case and I nearly got lost. And that was me mind you who thought he knew the place like the back of his hand. I can still remember thinking as I was driving around there that if you were looking for trouble this was the place to find it because it was waiting for you on every street corner. They should have still been in school, man – kids! Everyone of them with a knife in the back pocket. I don't know all the details about why Visagie was hanging on in Motherwell but I can tell you that it came as no surprise to me when I heard that he had been knifed. Ntloko says he heard from one of the Motherwell constables that Visagie was actually living in a pondok! If that is true then you got to ask yourself what the hell was really going on. Because you don't move into a Motherwell pondok for a little holiday my friend. I know the station there is treating it as just another township stabbing case, and I suppose they are right to do so because it does at least spare the family feelings and whatever he was up to he paid a pretty high price for it didn't he?

But you see I think if you was to dig a little bit there you would find a very different story to a simple township stabbing. And what about that letter which I heard they found in the pondok? Ja! A long one they say. They gave it to his wife. No, I am not prepared to say what I believe was going on but you can't tell me that Mr Visagie had moved into a Motherwell pondok for a little holiday specially as Shukuma happens to be one of the worst of the squatter camps in Motherwell. Read last week's newspaper and you'll see that 2 000 kilos of dagga were confiscated there in one week alone! Anyway it's not my case anymore so that's the end of it as far as I'm concerned.

I'm just sorry man I can't help you more to get to the bottom of this affair. In one of our chats he mentioned a fishing pal of his, Derek somebody-or-the-other – Derek Lawrence! You should talk to him. And while you are about it maybe also go over and see if his wife will talk to you. But be careful there – she's very bitter about it all.

KOEN VAN DEVENTER

Of course I remember him. But you want to know why? When most people come in here and find the missing person they is looking for there is usually a very sad emotion on their faces. Some of them cry their eyes out. I had one woman faint when she saw her dead husband's picture. Visagie laughed! You heard me right. Kept pointing to the picture of the dead woman – the woman he had killed mark you – and laughed like it was the funniest joke in the world.

Do you want to see it?

DEREK LAWRENCE

It was the strangest thing man because if there is one thing I can tell you without the shadow of a doubt it's that Roelfie knew what he was doing when he had a fishing rod in his hands. He might have made a mess up of everything else but when it came to this river and the chance of a Grunter or a Steenbras or a nice Kob then Roelf Visagie was one of the best. Thinking about it now I realise of course that that should have been a warning to me that he really was in trouble like Lorraine said, but you know how it is with friends, their wives are always complaining about them and then anyway Roelfie could be a really moody somebody when he felt like it.

But to get back to that night at Swartkops. I had passed out. It was one of those uncomfortable nights you see with an Easterly coming up from the mouth and because there's no shelter on the mud flats the only way to keep warm when it's like that is to bring out the bottle of slurpies – half and half – brandy and Coke. It's a traditional Swartkops remedy for keeping out the damp when you're waiting for some action at the end of your line. Roelfie had taken a couple of slugs from the bottle but I'm ashamed to say I knocked off three-quarters of it and then like I said I passed out. Now there's one thing you must know about a fisherman – he can be as poegaaid as your grandfather but if that ratchet starts screaming you are wide awake in a split bloody second and scrambling for your rod. I was no exception to the rule. I couldn't get my legs out of the sleeping bag but that made no bloody difference. When a Steenbras takes you like that – because that's the only fish that will get your reel screaming like that – you must waste no time and strike. Which is what I did only to realise that it wasn't my ratchet that was screaming but Roelfie's. But what really knocked me sideways is that he was just sitting there looking at the damned thing. The tip of his rod was all the way down man! It was kissing the water, his line peeling away from the reel and Roelfie was just sitting there looking at it. 'Wake up for Christ's sake Roelfie and strike the bugger!' He just looked at me as if I was the mad one. I scrambled over to his rod but – Ag! you know what happened – when I got it out of its holder the line was already limp as an old man's prick. That Steenbras got away. To fight another day, as they say.

So I asked him: 'Are you okay Roelfie?' Because he was just sitting there, looking at the water, as if nothing had happened.

'Ag ja wat, I'm okay.' And he laughed a little.

'Well you shouldn't be! Because you know what you just lost don't you?'

'What Derrie, what did I lose?'

'A fucking big, monster Steenbras my sweetheart, that is what. Five Ks — at least — my boeta.'

'Ja, that's a nice one alright. I'm glad.'

That's all. I'm glad. I was so the hell in I didn't know what to say after that. I just shoved his rod back in the holder and went back to look after mine. I had one of them out with live bait — I was hoping for Kob — and I was reeling it in to see if it was still okay when he looks at me and says:

'You know those times when you feel you've now really just had enough, when you're gat vol of the whole bloody mess and saying you wish you had never been born and so on and so forth. You ever go further than just feeling like that?'

I was still so the hell in so I only sort of half heard what he was saying. Quite frankly, the last thing I wanted at that moment was a long conversation about the meaning of life with my friend Roelfie. All I knew was that a big bloody Steenbras was laughing at us all the way down the river and I was hoping his big brother or a nice fat Kob would come along and pick me up for a change. But old Roelfie was somewhere else. He was going on about the meaning of this and the meaning of that and what's the purpose of anything and all that sort of bullshit so I close my ears and when I hear again it's about that Black woman and her name and I don't know what else. What I realise now of course is that if that Steenbras hadn't come along, and I had heard him properly, who knows, maybe ... You know what I mean? Maybe I would have realised what was going on in his head. That of course doesn't make me feel too good. But then you know I've also got a feeling that there was nothing nobody could have said that would have reached him. I'm not joking. When I think now about the way he was that night, then I'm telling you man if I had packed up my things and just left him there, he would have sat there and gone on talking to himself. I know it sounds crazy but I'm telling you that night there on the river Roelfie wasn't connected to anybody or anything anymore.

When?

If I remember correctly it was like a month or so after the accident. I had tried a couple of times already to get him to come out with me, but he wasn't interested. Then my wife Betty came home one day and said she had met Lorraine in Clicks and that Lorraine had begged her to ask me to take him fishing. 'I'm going mad with him in the house,' she said to Lorraine. So this time I drove around to his place with all my tackle loaded up, went into his garage and loaded his up and then went into the house and said 'You're coming with me and no argument. Get your arse into gear my friend.' And he did. Shame. Just before I got into the car Lorraine gave me a big squeeze and a 'Thank you Derrie'. So it goes hey.

I haven't been back to the river since then. I'm not superstitious or anything like that, but I think I've got to let a little bit of time pass before I throw a mud prawn into that river again. It's too close. We were friends for a long time. There's too many memories waiting for me down there. Specially when I hear a train. Mind you there's memories waiting for me at all the rivers – Gamtoos, Sundays, Bushmans, even up to the Kowie. We fished them all. Anyway, when I want to get my line wet these days I drive out to the Sundays River. But it's interesting you know. I was out there a couple of weeks ago. I pulled out a Grunter with my very first prawn – good pan size you know. I bait up again quickly and cast out. In the meantime the fish is flapping away next to me. Next thing I know is I've got my spare rod holder in my hand and – whack! – I put it out of its misery. That's what Roelfie always used to do. I don't personally think that fish have got feelings like us. I've even read somewhere that scientific experiments have proved that but even so I'm going to ask Lorraine for his moer stok for a keepsake. Sort of farewell gesture to him you know.

So there it. Sorry I can't tell you more.

LORAINE VISAGIE

You are not intruding. I am grateful for anyone who is prepared to listen to my side of the story.

Because you see what I want to know is what must I tell little Priscilla when she grows up and asks me: 'Where's my daddy, Mommy?' Nobody thinks about them do they, the ones that are left behind. Especially if they happen to be White! As it is we was barely making all our ends meet when he was alive, but now … I don't know what I am going to do. But of course this is now mos the brand New South Africa so will you please do all your crying for that poor Black drunk woman with the baby on her back who stood there in front of my husband's train and just forget about me and my babies. Of course she was drunk! What mother in her right mind would do a thing like that? Drink and dagga! Sies! Don't ask me to cry for her Argentina. We all know those days when you just feel you've had enough. I had plenty of them myself believe me in my years with Roelf Visagie! But it's your baby that brings you back to earth — makes you realise you got to make a go of it, not the other way around. Children aren't to blame for the bloody mess we grown ups make of our lives.

What it comes down to, and I am going to talk frankly now, is that the government is to blame. Yes! They must take responsibility for the whole bloody mess — that woman, Roelf, the breakup of our marriage — everything! And it's not just us. Look at the mess the country is in. And this, mind you, is supposed to be the New South Africa. I think it might have worked if old Mandela had stayed around a little longer, but this new crowd? Not even that old Tutu gives them a chance anymore. I am not saying the Black people shouldn't be given their share of everything but why the hurry for God's sake like the world was going to end tomorrow. You can't rush something like that. It's like trying to eat all your food at once. And what happens then? Indigestion. That is what this country is suffering from now. Indigestion. You see as far as me and the kids was concerned everything was going to be alright. Of course we was all upset for him when he told us what had happened and I specially could see he was holding a lot of things inside him. I mean you can't live with somebody for fifteen years and not know something about what's going on inside them, not so? But as Miss Conradie herself said to me it's not the first time that somebody has stood on a railway line to end it all and it won't be the last. When I think about it now I suppose the nightmares he was having should have been some sort of a warning to me but there again you see Miss Conradie said it would take him a little time to get over it and that I must just be patient and carry on as normal.

Anyway it was because of the nightmares that he moved to the pull-out in the lounge. Don't let anybody tell you I kicked him out of the bed. It was his idea so that I could at least get some sleep. I've got to start very early for my job at Clicks and he could sleep late because they gave him sick-leave. But apart from that it looked as if we was in for just another happy Christmas until of course we get to the night he smashed the Christmas tree. I still go cold and skrik when I think about it now. I don't think I have ever had such a big fright in my life! Just imagine it, the house is quiet, the children are asleep and so am I, all of us in dreamland until suddenly there is a noise, a bang or an explosion or I don't know what and we are all awake with our hearts in our mouths. Obviously I think there are burglars in the house smashing everything and I rush to the children's room. Then we hear that the noise is coming from the lounge and we can hear Roelfie swearing so I think he is fighting with the burglars so I run to the door to help him and what do I see? He is fighting alright but not with the burglars. It's the Christmas tree he's got in his hands and smashing to the ground again and again and again. That's a mad man wouldn't you say? I did. I said it to the children and I said it to Miss Conradie when I went to see her the next day to report what happened. I think she almost didn't believe me at first because she also had no idea that he was so close to boiling point inside. She told me to tell him to come in and see her immediately and in all fairness to Roelfie he did that. I could see him try once again to carry on as usual. He bought another Christmas tree even though it was by now nearly the New Year. He watched television with the kids and he even went fishing with Derek one night. But this time I was on my guard. Miss Conradie had warned me that if there was any sign of violence again to clear out with the children. I had it all arranged with my sister in Newton Park. But as you maybe know it was Roelfie that cleared out. Not a word, not a telephone call, nothing! To be honest with you because it was now so nice and quiet in the house again with just me and the kids I didn't think to report anything. I thought it best to just wait and see what happens but then the next thing I know is that the police at Motherwell location is on the telephone asking me if he is missing and when I said yes they said they think they had found him and would I please go to the Morgue next to the Police Station to identify his body.

And this is what they give me after they found him dead there in the slum. They found it in the pondok that people said he was living in. Can you imagine the disgrace to me and my children. Do you know what the neighbours are saying? What the other children are saying at school? And all this talk about the 'mystery' of Roelf Visagie. There's no mystery. He was sleeping with a Black woman. I told the police: 'Go find that woman and you'll solve your "mystery".' That's what happens to an Afrikaner man when he goes mad. He runs to a Black woman. Remember all the dominees who got arrested in the old days? Thank God my mother died last year because if she had been alive today this whole mess would have killed her.

I've tried reading this but I stopped after a few pages. It's all rubbish about him and some old Black man he met. Roelfie was mad at the end. You can read it if you want to. I can't make any sense of it.

SIMON HANABE

All I see is that Mr Mdoda bring him to Boplaas. Mr Mdoda give me some work digging graves for him there and I was digging. And then he comes with the White man. When Mr Mdoda goes the White man walks around looking, looking, looking at all the graves.

So I finish my job and I go. We didn't talk. That is all I see.

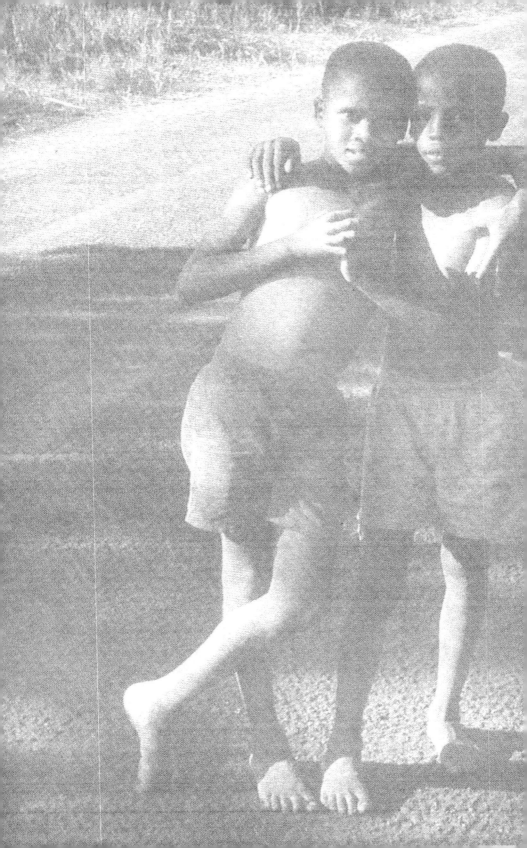